PARCHED

A VAMPIRE ROMANTASY SERIES

PARCHED
BOOK ONE

Z. L. ARKADIE

FLAMING HEARTS PRESS MEDIA LLC

ISBN: 978-1-942857-57-0

❀ Formatted with Vellum

This book is dedicated to my Mother, my first editor, beta reader and fan. Love you dearly, Mom.

ONE

I can barely see past my nose. The fog rolled in before dawn—thick, unnatural, swallowing the skyline whole. By the time I left for work, Manhattan looked like a city holding its breath. Maybe that's just me. Maybe it's the shoes.

I stop long enough to wiggle my toes. My feet are already aching inside my Manolo Blahnik Mary Jane heels. I can blame my mom, Freda, for them. When I landed my job at Lang, Bender & Jenison Advertising, she sent over a fifty-piece wardrobe, complete with shoes, and a note that read, *You need to look the part of an executive selling beauty products, Clarity.*

Naturally, I was offended.

I can never tell what she's thinking, but that

note didn't require interpretation. The real me wasn't enough.

On my first day, I showed up in a black pantsuit I thought was refined, airy, and perfectly appropriate, along with a black turtleneck because I love the way they nestle against my neck. It didn't take long to realize Freda had been right. People questioned my competence. Someone even used the word "slob."

The next morning, I wore the designer clothes. Suddenly everyone assumed I knew what I was talking about when it came to beauty and fashion.

I didn't need the wardrobe to do my job well. But I have to admit, looking the part made things easier. The clothes, I've adjusted to. But the shoes? Never.

I wiggle my toes again and sigh. The day has barely started and my feet are already on fire. Thankfully, my building is less than a block away. I pull myself together and keep walking, the fog curling around my ankles as if it's trying to follow me inside.

That's ridiculous.

Still, it feels thicker than usual. Heavy. Pressing.

I step through the revolving doors with the other early arrivals and wait for the elevator. Three familiar faces from the office stand nearby. They avoid eye contact, but I know they're aware of me. I know because I can feel them.

I've always had abilities. I can sense emotions, hear thoughts, and sometimes—if I'm not careful—I slip too far inside someone else's head. I don't just understand them. I become the full embodiment of who they are. Their insecurities. Their jealousy. Their private hungers.

No real human being should be able to do that. But I can. Even as a child, I could.

So I'm aware that the cold shoulder this morning isn't subtle. It's about my father—Felix Parker, a major investor in the firm. No matter how much I prove myself, some people will always believe nepotism carved my seat at the table. Maybe it opened the door. Results kept me there.

When the partners made me executive director of Fashion and Beauty two months after I graduated from Harvard Business School, they had their doubts. Felix insisted I was qualified. They reluctantly agreed. Within a year, I put Lang, Bender & Jenison on the map. Clients ask for me by name.

That doesn't make me well liked.

As the elevator rises, I'm forced to feel my colleagues' resentment pressing in on all sides. It's like standing in a room where the air is slightly off. Tainted. And beneath it—just faintly—there's something else. A current I don't recognize. By the time the elevator doors open, the feeling is gone.

I hurry toward my office, eager to shut the door on other people's thoughts, but Michael Colton's executive assistant catches up to me.

"Miss Parker?"

She calls me that because she thinks I'm uptight.

I smile. "Feel free to call me Clarity."

"Yes, right. Clarity." She adjusts her folder. "Michael would like you to prepare brand contact and media objectives and present them to the Red Yard executives tonight at the Waldorf."

The request hits me harder than it should.

"Red Yard?" I ask. "The energy drink?"

"Yes. They asked for you specifically."

Specifically.

"Is there a strategy meeting scheduled this afternoon?"

"No. Tonight's meant to be impromptu. Casual."

Casual?

At the Waldorf?

I close my eyes for a moment and take a slow

breath. When I open them, Leona's anxiety flickers across my senses, but it's layered with something else—anticipation.

"Okay," I say finally. "I'll see what I can come up with."

She leaves, and I don't feel peaceful.

I sit at my desk and power up my computer. By ten o'clock, I've pulled up the Red Yard proposal folder on the cloud and am still scanning for angles that might justify this last-minute demand.

"Morning, Clarity."

I look up to see Barbara Ready, my assistant, in the doorway, holding a white paper bag and coffee. I can already smell bacon, eggs, and cheese tucked inside a sweet croissant.

"Morning," I say, though I don't sound it.

"Red Yard got you tied in knots?"

She doesn't have to read my face. My thoughts are loud enough.

"This is strange, don't you think?" I tap my fingers against the desk. "Projects like this usually go to Sanford. And you know how he gets when anyone infringes on his territory—especially me."

Barbara flops onto the leather sofa along the wall. *Just like her to torpedo a good thing*, she thinks.

I stiffen slightly.

Reading minds makes the social aspect of my job exhausting. It's hard to engage in polite conversation when you know exactly what someone is thinking. It's harder still when men are imagining things they would never say aloud.

"I'll call Michael," I say. "Maybe we can brainstorm and he can take the ideas to the client without me."

"He was adamant about you attending," Barbara replies. *And why didn't you tell me sooner?*

"Sorry," I say.

"About what?"

"Not telling you about tonight. I forgot."

She studies me, still unsettled by how often I anticipate her thoughts. "I can go with you," she offers. "If you want."

There's sacrifice in her energy. She has plans tonight. A friend's birthday party she's been looking forward to.

"No," I say quickly. "I'll handle it."

She nods but doesn't leave.

"Clarity… can I ask you something?"

I brace myself. "Sure."

"Why are you so… wary about these events? All you have to do is hold a cocktail and pretend the conversation's interesting. After a few drinks, anything is."

If only she knew alcohol makes me sick.

I glance toward the window. The fog hasn't lifted. If anything, it's thickened, dulling the edges of the skyline.

I don't know why I have the anxiety," I admit. "But maybe tonight's a good time to work on it." And I mean what I say. I really do want to try, kick this weakness of mine in the bud. I will climb the ladder faster if I strengthen my social game.

She smiles as if satisfied. "That's the right attitude."

BY LATE AFTERNOON, MICHAEL STILL HASN'T returned my calls. At six-thirty, the breakfast sandwich remains untouched on my desk.

I swivel in my chair and stare out at the city lights glowing through the fog. They look distant and distorted.

For a brief second, I feel it again. Not office politics. Not ambition. Not jealousy. It's something older. Something that doesn't feel human at all.

Then the sensation disappears, leaving only the hum of traffic below.

I sigh, shut down my computer, grab my purse, and sling it over my shoulder. I stand, gazing out the window, and all there is to see is bleak whiteness. And for the first time today, I'm not sure the fog is the only thing waiting for me outside.

CHAPTER

TWO

R iding down the elevator alone, I assess myself in the silver walls. I'm too tall, and I have too much hair. Regardless, I free my locks out of the bun and dig the red lipstick out from the bottom of my purse. By the time the door opens, I've fluffed out my curls, applied lipstick, and dropped the tube back into my purse. I glance at myself one more time and try to ignore the striking image I see looking back at me. The way I look is unreal, just like my abilities.

Suddenly I'm struck by a memory of the first time I tried to cut my hair. I was fifteen years old. Freda was on location in New York for a lead actress role in a prime-time miniseries, and Felix was in New Delhi acquiring a software company from venture capitalists. I was at home in Bel Air with Aries, the nanny who loved to wear coral-blue dashikis and turquoise jewelry and make out with her boyfriend, Raz.

It was a hot July afternoon when I stepped onto the patio with my hair sheared. Raz, a beachy-looking surfer dude with long, messy blond hair, had just taken three jumps on the edge of the diving board and dove headfirst into the blue dolphin-shaped pool. Aries sat on the opposite end, watching him with a bright smile. Her mocha skin glistened in the sun. After a hoot and holding up eight fingers to score his dive, Aries turned to look at me with my hair all gone.

"Hey, Clarity," she called all cool, calm and collected. "Did you see that? He thinks he's in the Olympics!" Then she laughed.

That was the extent of her reaction. I went to bed that night wondering what my parents would think and if I was really that invisible to the people in my life. Then something eerie happened. By the end of the week, my hair had grown back to the same length—spiraling all the way to the small of my back and as thick as cotton candy.

On Friday morning, all Aries said to me was, "Good morning, Clarity. You want to hang out with

us today? It's hot, so we're hitting the beach."
Again, she behaved as if she hadn't noticed that my
hair had grown back in less than five days.

I tried cutting it again when I turned twenty-
one, and once again, it grew back in one week.
After that, I swore I was never cutting it again. I
don't think about those two terrifying incidents
anymore. Out of sight, out of mind. Now, every
morning, I twist my tresses up into a tight bun just
above the nape of my neck, and voila, there's my
haircut.

ON MY WALK TO THE WALDORF, I'M BEATEN UP BY
the thoughts and feelings of strangers. No one is
relaxed; everyone is anxious about the tasks they
have to complete before bedtime. As usual, their
worries are transferred to me, sending my nerves
into a tizzy.

Finally, I'm standing under the golden marquee
of the Waldorf Astoria Hotel. I take a deep breath,
hoping the oxygen will infuse me with confidence. It
does for the moment, so I head inside.

In the lobby, the decor is lemon gold and very
elegant. I want to turn around and leave, but

instead I follow familiar faces down a short staircase to the ballroom. Faint music fills the air. It's a wiry contemporary instrumental. The notes twist and turn into a striking falsetto and then repeat. The lights are dim, but everything sparkles. The sconces attached to the walls, the bulky stone pillars, the sparkling vases, and the potted plants are all aglow. I'm the only woman in a suit. My female colleagues are in strappy cocktail dresses.

I catch sight of the marketing team, then sales, my copywriters, accounts, and finally the other creative directors. Most of the attendees are grouped in threes or fours, sipping cocktails out of sexy glasses and chatting. They all see me, especially my copywriters. They all have the same old comments. I'm ready to hear something new about myself.

Look who the rain dragged in.

Wonder how long she'll stay.

She wore that suit today? She could've at last tried.

Ah, Clarity Parker, maybe I'll strike up a convo later.

She's so damn hot.

She's so damn odd.

What the hell is she doing here?

That's the comment I follow. It leads directly to Sanford Giles, who's part of a circle, standing with the bigwigs. He's hoping I do an about-face and leave. I'm contemplating making his wishes come true when Michael Colton catches a glimpse of me.

He waves me over. "Clarity!"

His cohorts study me with shining, expectant eyes. He's entertaining a select bunch. Along with Sanford, executive creative director of Consumable Products, there's Peter Root, VP of Major Accounts, Douglas McCarthy, VP of Marketing, and Greg Long, one of the named partners. I've never seen them so happy to see me. I sense greed as the primary motivator. Peter Root is appraising me. For some reason, he's trying to figure out what some person he's calling "he" sees in me, and he's trying to find it from my legs up to my face. There's no escaping, so I walk over. The men make space next to Michael.

"It's good to see you here," Michael says as his hand comes down on my shoulder and squeezes.

"Well, I got the memo, so…"

"Yes, yes," he says passively, glossing over the fact that although I'm here, I'm not happy about it. "So." The word hangs in the air for a moment, signaling all eyes back on him. "Red Yard wants to saturate the market at a record pace."

He's looking at me. They all are, and now I'm shrinking into my aching feet. I'll definitely take a cab home.

"Baron Ford," he says and pauses to read how familiar I am with that name.

I nod stiffly to give no indication that I know exactly who he is. I'm shocked to hear that name in this setting, at this stage of my life—far away from Cambridge, Massachusetts, and over five years later.

THREE

WHO'S BARON FORD?

I came to be a lover of downtown living during my six-year stint in Cambridge, Massachusetts—four years at Harvard University and then two at the Harvard Business School. The best part of each was being far away from my parents' already distant reach. Freda didn't care much for any towns in Massachusetts beyond Martha's Vineyard and Cape Code—places she called solid vacation destinations. My dad, Felix, only rode into town on business. Unlike my mother, he didn't do lunch or dinner with daughter. Even now, my father never calls to check how my day went or learn if I'm happy or sad. He has only a few self-appointed purposes in my life. Felix keeps my bank account stacked. He makes sure I follow the path he sets for me, and insists that I only live in places he selects.

That's how I came to live in the Bend Condominiums, smack-dab in the middle of Cambridge. I loved that place, the whimsical building that tilted a little. Architect Vick Moyers had the Leaning Tower of Pisa and Big Ben in mind when he drafted the plans. I occupied the penthouse, which had seven master suites with bathrooms attached. It also had two dens, a living room, and a humungous kitchen. All the furniture was contemporary chic, my dad's favorite style: straight chairs; hard, red fabric sofas; white marble floors; crystal glass tables; furry white area rugs; lots of metal and wooden shelves. Everything was spotless, well-ordered, and stylish, just the way Felix likes it.

But for me, the ambiance of the condo was so cold that on most days, it literally gave me chills. One day, I sat on one of those stiff sofas and stared out at the city. To my surprise, a feeling of warmth hugged me. There's something fascinating about how man-made structures shoot up toward a gaping sky. Those buildings have souls, stories, yet I'm unable to hear their innermost thoughts or feel their feelings. What I see is all I get. That's what I liked. I always hoped I could experience other people in that same way, but I never could.

Back then, I spent a lot of time in the eighteenth-floor lounge. The sofas there were different from the ones inside my condo. They were the gigantic, cushiony sorts. On many nights, I actually fell asleep on them. They were brown and velvety, and the floor was covered with actual shag carpet. I used to take my shoes off to let my toes play in the fibers. I always wanted carpet. When Freda and Felix divorced, I thought, one of them would finally get a place with carpet, but unfortunately, their disdain for floor fibers is one of a handful of things they have in common.

On the day I met Baron Ford, it was pouring rain. The clouds hovered like sooty smokestacks, and a stinging chill sat in the air. My first class started at ten in the morning, and my last class ended at five. I was walking home on the damp path that rounded Soldier's Field with my waterproof backpack slung over my shoulder when I happened to glance right for no apparent reason, and saw a flyer pinned to a bulletin board. Written in black ink on wet canary yellow paper was "God, The First Sculptor, 5:30 p.m., Hall 'A' Science Center, Dr. Herbert Dove."

I didn't stop to study the flyer. As a matter of fact, I kept moving because I couldn't wait to get home, dig out my sketch pad, and sketch in the lounge. I'm an artist at heart; I make sculptures. I had planned to work on "Heart of Mine," a piece I'd been conceiving. But before I reached the main street, freezing fog, so thick I could hardly see my hand in front of my face, rolled in out of nowhere. My plan to gaze out at the lit skyscrapers while sketching had been thwarted. So I chose to find my way to the Science Center and sit in on the guest lecturer's seminar instead.

WHEN I ARRIVED, DR. DOVE, A MAN WITH shoulder length white hair and a very youthful face, had already taken the podium. Nearly every seat was occupied. Normally, those talks weren't so crowded, but I later learned that Dr. Dove had a following.

I spotted one empty chair between a tall man with blond, neck-length hair and a brunette who kept glancing at him with a flirtatious grin. I looked around for another seat, not wanting to thwart her romantic assault, but the chair between them was my best option. I crawled over ten sets of knees, and when I finally made it to the seat, I fell into it with a sigh of relief. That was when I accidentally elbowed the blond guy.

"Sorry," I muttered with a glance at him.

I did a double take, instantly taken aback by his all consuming good looks and something else I picked up from him. He had a very strange drive, a deep desire to have my soul, my body, and, strangely, my blood. What threw me off even more was that I yearned to satisfy his craving.

Dr. Dove was in the middle of describing how God had parted water from surfaces and formed the planets when I realized the guy seated next to me and I were still staring at each other. The man had the face of a beautiful barbarian. Who looked like that? High forehead, angled chin, shallow beard, piercing topaz eyes. He looked menacing and harmless at the same time. He was pale, very pale. However, his skin was stunning against his soft, pink lips that were the sort my clients, who are in the cosmetic business, liked to use to sell lipstick.

I was about to get up and move as far away from him as possible but then something that I spent years praying for had happened: I could no longer read his thoughts or feel his emotions.

"What's your name?" he asked. There was a strange, animalistic growl in the back of his throat.

"Clarity," I said before realizing maybe I shouldn't have shared that bit of information with him.

"Clarity, get out of here—now," he said through clenched teeth. "The fog isn't safe."

My chest felt as if it had stopped beating. He hadn't made much sense at all, but something had triggered deep inside me, and I believed him. But it was more than that—I sensed the danger he warned me about. Something evil was hunting me. It wasn't him, though. I checked both shoulders. Nothing. Not yet. I didn't bother trying to understand what it all meant. I shot to my feet, pushed past those ten pairs of knees without saying excuse me, and rushed out into the bitterly cold fog.

I don't remember how I got home. I let my instincts guide me. Walt, the doorman, was already holding the door open when I got close. Once I was in the lobby, I stared out into the night as the white vapor rubbed against the glass.

"It's scary out there, isn't it?" Walt asked.

"Yeah, it is," I whispered, really studying how strangely thick the mist was.

"Well, don't go back out there tonight. It's safer inside."

"Don't I know it."

I wondered why and how I knew it. And who was that guy at the seminar? Why was I so attracted to him, attached to him. Suddenly out of breath, I realized at that very moment that he and I were somehow bonded.

FOUR

After a long night's sleep, I woke up brave and thinking I'd never see the strange man with the seductive energy again. That revelation also had a lot to do with the fact that I had a final project due Friday, so I had no time to think about the crazy incident. I spent the day in my home office, arranging my data, typing out my results, and making calls to my team members to make sure we were all on the same page. My classmates were amazed at how easy all of it was for me, which in turn made it easy for them.

At sundown, I shut down my laptop, snatched my sketch pad off the top shelf of my closet, and headed down to the eighteenth-floor lounge. Yesterday's fog was gone, and a bright full moon lingered behind thin layers of clouds. The effect was haunting. I'd gotten the evening I had hoped for.

I was an hour into sketching when an uneasy feeling gripped me. I remember watching my frozen hand, afraid to turn to see who was standing in my peripheral vision.

"I thought I'd seen you somewhere before," a man said.

That's when I turned to see the same guy from the seminar, the guy who warned me to leave, the guy who wanted to consume me. I whipped around to glance over both sides of my shoulders. We were all alone. I was scared stiff.

"You live here?" I asked, blinking at the contours of his attractive face.

He cracked a tiny smile and sat on the other side of the sofa. "You're Clarity Parker?"

I frowned. "Yes."

"Yes," he said.

"Yes what?"

"Yes, I live here."

Why can't I hear or feel him? "But how do you know my name?"

He continued staring at my face as if each of my features was a bright new discovery.

"I asked," he finally said.

"Who?"

His gaze fell to my lips and then stopped at my neck. "Walt," he barely said and then took hard swallow.

"Oh," I said, finding his answer reasonable.

I decided to break eye contact and start drawing again.

"You're an artist?" he asked.

When I looked up at him, he was still staring at me in that intense manner. It made me uncomfortable enough to glance over my shoulder, hoping someone, anyone would walk in. No one did, so I flipped the pad closed.

"I have to go," I mumbled and shot out of there so fast, for a moment I thought I was actually, *like actually*, floating on air.

However, from that point on, every evening at eight p.m., Baron Ford would come into the lounge and sit on the opposite end of my favorite sofa to read Market Watch or Business Insider. His energy felt engrossing. I could've chosen to remain in my condo and sketch, but I had to admit that I liked seeing him, experiencing his nearness. For a few days, we never said a word to each other. I trained myself to focus on my sketching and ignore him altogether.

Then, one evening, out of the blue, he said, "Baron Ford."

I looked up from page. His eyes were just as intense as they always were.

"Sorry?" I asked, sounding a little distracted. Gosh he looked good, and smelled good too. He wore dark blue jeans that fit him perfectly and a navy blue button-down shirt with a solid white T-shirt beneath it. The garments were expensive and well made, as if he'd been dressed by Freda herself.

He smirked. "That's my name. You never asked. Thought you should know it."

His face went through a lot of extraordinary contortions to reveal his thoughts, but my favorite was his smirk. It's still branded in my memory.

"Oh," was all I could say. My mind went blank, which wasn't a normal state for me.

"I thought you were a business major, but you're always drawing," he said, pointing his chin at my pad.

"Oh," I stupidly said again.

That was a loaded moment. My brain took off into four different directions. I had a number of responses, but none of them would form into words.

"You don't talk much, either."

"I talk," I croaked, sort of not wanting our interaction to cease.

He got up and walked to the window. I think we both were watching the glowing red letters that spelled out *The Centre* until he glanced over his shoulder to look at me. "Do you like that?"

"Like what?"

"The view. It's what you observe whenever you take a break from your drawing. But you do more than examine it, it inspires you."

His back side was equal to his front. He was a few inches over six feet tall and built like an athlete. His voice was like velvet wrapped around thunder. Everything about him added up to objective perfection. However, now that I look back, I think that I also liked being around him because he was silent. I couldn't hear his thoughts or feel his emotions. At times I forcefully tried, but still, it felt as if a wall made of steel kept him from me.

"Yeah, I love the view," I said.

"What about me?" he asked.

"What do you mean?"

He faced me. "What do you think about me?"

His gaze held me captive. "I don't know you."

He sat down beside me like he had two weeks ago—very close. "Not my fault."

"Not your fault?"

"It's not my fault you don't know me. I sit here every night, and you don't say anything."

"Well, you don't say anything to me, either," I blurted.

He stared deep into my eyes and leaned in closer. "I'm saying something now."

My expression remained blank. Was he coming on to me? Did he want to date me? Did he want to kiss me? Then I thought maybe I was assuming too much too soon.

"I guess you are," I whispered.

He sniffed, chuckling. Goodness, I loved his face. I was undeniably attracted to him—acutely attracted to him. We smiled at each other, and then he returned to reading the Business Insider and I continued sketching. But it was how comfortably we existed in those quiet moments that spooked me.

Baron Ford and I didn't quite date from that moment forward. I didn't know how to be forward about matters of the heart, and he apparently respected the invisible boundary I put up. The thought of going on an actual date with him scared the living daylights out of me, but we spoke every night in the lounge. He asked me interesting questions about myself. He once asked me if I knew my origins and how many of me there were.

"Just one, I think," I answered with a laugh. "Why? Do you think I have a twin or something?"

He didn't return my laugh. He looked away, frustrated about something. "You don't know, do you?"

"No, I don't," I said with a hint of cynicism. My laughter simmered. "Please enlighten me."

He simply smiled. Damn it I wished I could read him.

"What do you plan to do after you graduate?" he asked instead.

The answer was easy. "Work for my father."

"Felix Parker?"

My eyebrows ruffled. "You know him?"

"You can't be in business and not know Felix Parker?"

True. "Then you're in business?"

"Yes. I am."

I loved how honest his answer sounded.

After we said good-bye for the night, after I took a long, hot shower, drank a cup of hot peppermint tea, listened to the beginnings of a message from

Freda, and crawled into bed, it dawned on me how truly out there his question about how many of me are out there was.

The next night I didn't show up to draw in the lounge. My day ran late because I had to finish proofreading my thesis before printing it out, binding it and running it down to Dr. Ramsey's office. By the time I got home, all I wanted to do was make a cup of peppermint tea, pull the curtains, and sit in the dark. I planned to enjoy the peace, but then the doorbell chimed. My back stiffened. I never had company.

I walked cautiously to the door and peeked through the peephole. Baron looked into my eyes, waving. My heart fluttered, and I stepped back, shocked.

"Hey," I called.

"Hey," he said, sounding more like velvet than thunder.

I didn't say anything for a few seconds. One would think that a person as smart as I am would come up with something better than, "What do you want?"

"Do you have a few hours?"

Again, I looked through the peephole.

Again, he waved at me. "So is this how you talk to your callers?"

That was when it hit me that we were actually talking through wood. I opened the door. He stood in a pair of dark pants and a white crisp, button-down shirt. Clearly he wasn't planning to spend those few hours inside my place.

"Sorry," I said with a grin, definitely affected by his appearance. "I'm just um…"

Why does he look at me that way? I was certain he wasn't aware of how his gaze pulled me apart, tinkered with my insides and left me breathless. His eyes always dissected me. Never in my life had I wanted to know what a person felt and thought more than that moment.

He graced me with his smoldering smirk. "Are you going to wear that? Because I don't mind?"

I had on a royal blue tank dress. I crossed my arms once his gaze reminded me I wasn't wearing a bra.

I glanced down at the comfy socks on my feet. "I wasn't planning on going anywhere. But where do you want to take me?"

"Just come with me and see," he replied still simpering. Gosh, he was such a remarkable flirt.

Then I did something I rarely do. I chuckled. "What?"

"Go ahead, get dressed. I dare you to join me."

The way he said that made my sex flutter. The sensation was odd. My lust for him nonsensical.

Of course, I ended up slipping on a little black wrap dress by DVF, Freda swore it made me look unrivaled, with black boots. I wavered between wearing my hair up or down, I went with down. The truth was, I wanted to impress him. I was in the habit of playing my looks down, but on that night, I wanted Baron Ford to be utterly enthralled by me. So I fluffed out my mane and presented my best self to him.

"You're very beautiful and sexy, Clarity," he whispered thickly when I met him at the door.

"Thanks," I said, shying away from the intensity in his eyes and that delicious sensation in my lady parts.

He held out his hand. "Are you ready?"

"Yes." I took his hand, and the most amazing thing happened—my entire body warmed up. It was as if the perfect seventy-eight-degree day was contained inside me.

I knew he felt it too because we stood staring at

each other for a few heartbeats before walking off in a daze.

FIVE

B aron took me to a nude sculpture exhibit in East Cambridge at a gallery along the Charles River. He held my hand the whole time. I only realized that I left my coat at home when he let go of my hand to open the door for me. However, when I took his hand again, the chill faded from every part of my body. It was a strange phenomenon, sort of like not being able to hear his thoughts or feel his emotions, but I was too captivated by him to be alarmed by it.

As we strolled through the gallery, I felt like I was floating on air. He spoke with his face close to mine, asking me what I liked or disliked about each piece we encountered. He listened to me explain texture, line, curve, and shadow and how the effects evoked emotion.

I was so wrapped up in him that I didn't notice how dark the general atmosphere was and how many of the attendees were eyeing us suspiciously until we were about an hour in. We were on the third level, examining a murky ice sculpture carved into a cloaked being with a skeletal face, when he pulled me against his hard body.

"Let's go." His whisper was full of alarm.

Before I could say anything, we were on our way down the stairs. He was moving very fast, but I was somehow able to keep up with him. I kept searching around us for someone equivalent to a slighted girlfriend. At the moment, it was the most logical explanation.

"What's going on?" I asked once we were out in a bitter cold night that I still couldn't feel.

"It was nothing." He glanced over both shoulders. "Just some people I'd rather not see."

"People or person? Like a girlfriend?" I asked bluntly.

We were still moving too fast. He held my hand as we weaved effortlessly past others.

"I don't have a girlfriend, Clarity."

I swallowed a gasp. He didn't say those words

out loud. Finally, and for a fleeting instance, I was able to hear his thoughts.

"What did you say?" I finally asked.

"It's business," he said.

I paused. "Legal or illegal?"

He chuckled, amused. "Are you asking if I'm a criminal?"

I tilted me head slightly. "Are you?"

His gaze enslaved me. "No."

"Okay," I said past my tight throat.

"I don't want to share your attention with anyone else tonight, that's all," he said.

Gosh, I never felt so special. Why didn't he kiss me then? He should've kissed me then.

We ended up walking across the Longfellow Bridge to spot boats passing under the arches in the hazy purple night. For the longest time, we didn't say a word. We simply enjoyed the quenching feeling of being near each other.

"I forgot what warmth felt like," Baron said, breaking the silence.

He squeezed my hand before pulling me against him, his front side against my backside. My body quivered with a lust so intense that it scared me to death.

"What's happening between us?" I asked

breathlessly.

He spun me around to face him, and our mouths melted. Our kissing was warm and tender. His tongue tasted delicious. My head floated and spun at the same time.

"Do you believe in myths?" he whispered.

My lidded gaze held his. "What kind of myths?"

His lips parted. Suddenly, I could sense him wondering if I could feel his breath. I tried. I couldn't.

"Any myth. Just think of one," he said.

"Unicorns?"

He chuckled lightly. "Do you believe in unicorns?"

"No." I pressed my lips, thinking about my ability. "Maybe."

Baron raised his eyebrows. "Maybe?"

I wondered if I should tell him. Reveal who I truly am. *But who am I?*

Then, his lips claimed mine again. Slow and deep our tongues dove into each other's mouths. I found myself craving more, needing more from him. I wanted his manhood inside me. I wanted his passion to fill me, set me on fire. That's when I realized how much I was shivering. My lust scared me and I pulled away from him.

Detached from his touch, the cold gripped me.

I folded my arms, hugging myself. "Why am I warm when I touch you and cold when I don't."

His lips parted but he spoke no words. Again, I couldn't penetrate his thoughts, which made me wonder if he knew how to deliberately keep me out of his head. Who was this man that I was so desperately attracted to? Did he already know my secrets?

"It's getting late. I should get home," I said. The stifling cold was making me uncomfortable so I reached out to take his hand.

As soon as our limbs connected, the chill faded. I couldn't fool myself. It was our touching that kept me warm on an icy night. And the reason for that phenomenon was probably just as frightening as my abilities.

CHAPTER

SIX

We walked back to our building in silence. But inside me, something scarier was happening. I wanted him to make love to me. No... I wanted him to ravish me, to make love to me like nobody ever has before. I could tell he wanted it too. I could feel it when he pressed himself against me.

We were close to my building when he said, "I'm sorry if I upset you."

I shook my head. "No, it's more than likely not you. I'm just not very trusting, and I don't know what you really want from me."

He paused and pulled me close. "As I said, and it's a fact, I like you, Clarity. In a very, very, unique way."

"It takes more than one date to know if you like someone, doesn't it?" I was falling fast for him too, and that made me just as unreasonable.

"Not if it was meant to be."

I thought maybe he's right. In a strange way, maybe he, the man who warns me, was a missing piece to my odd existence. That's when I decided to let down my guard and heave caution to the wind. We made out some more; the act filled me with that strange warmth. I felt as if I was outside of myself during all of our heavy petting and deep kissing.

When we finally reached my front door, it was after three in the morning. We stood facing each other, and I pondered step two. I wasn't a virgin, but I wasn't the sort of girl who engaged in sex frequently.

I'd lost my virginity during my senior year as an undergrad. Jessie Langston was his name, and I just wanted to do it because I wondered if I could have sex. I was twenty-one and hadn't even started my period yet. I thought having sex would help with that. I heard the first time hurt like hell, but I didn't feel anything at all. It was like he wasn't inside me. I wondered if it would be the same with Baron.

Baron looked into my eyes, wearing that small smirk I was sure he used to hypnotize me. I was on the verge of inviting him inside when my door swung open.

At first, I thought we were standing in front of the wrong condo, but I finally recognized the lady with orange-brown hair cut into multiple layers. The color wasn't flattering against her chestnut skin. And I was pretty sure, in that moment, her brown eyes glowed yellow.

"Mom?" I asked, shocked beyond words to see her.

Baron stepped back, and they exchanged angry glances. The confrontation was short but long enough for me to notice.

"What are you doing?"—she snapped, still glaring at him. Then she directed her glare at me to ask—"out this late?"

A flood of thoughts ran through my mind as I watched my mother. Like, why is Freda in Cambridge? And why did she arrive without calling? When I remembered I wasn't alone and thought I should at least officially introduce Baron to my mother, I turned to face him, and he was gone.

I couldn't believe it. "Where did he go?"

"I don't care, and you shouldn't either," Freda

said sharply. I pulled my head back in shock. "What?" I had never heard her be so rude.

Then she forced a fake smile. "I meant, if he didn't want to stick around, then he's not worthy of you."

Narrowing my eyes, I studied her. I could never read her thoughts or feel her emotions. The same goes for my father. It's an odd thing. I always concluded it's because they're the two humans, maybe they're humans, who made me.

"Right," I whispered, even though I didn't believe her at all.

Nevertheless, that was the last time I saw or heard from Baron Ford.

SEVEN

PRESENT

I can hardly believe Baron Ford is somewhere, wandering around this huge ballroom. The head guys are still staring at me, trying to discern how well I know the phantom who stepped in and out of my life five years ago. My expression remains as undiscerning as a rock, but I have to say something, and then get out of here as fast as I can.

I put on my most affable smile. "Apologies, gentlemen, I didn't have an opportunity to jot down ideas for Red Yard today, as I was told about the account last minute. But tomorrow I can put together a brief report."

Breathe, concentrate. I'm listening to Michael's thoughts. He wants me here. Since Baron was so adamant about me handling his account, Michael suspects he and I had an affair, and he wants to view our reactions when we see each other.

"That's fine," he says, "but I want to introduce you to Baron Ford while you're here."

I put my hand on his shoulder. "Sorry, but I must excuse myself."

She must excuse herself, Michael thinks.

Everything spins as I walk away. I feel as if what I'm running from is chasing me. Still, there's no sign of Baron Ford anywhere. As I swerve through groups of chatterers, I wonder if he's seen me already. All my senses are heightened, so words and emotions penetrate me, stabbing me deep. I won't stop moving. *I'm so out of here*. What is Michael going to do, fire me? He can't. Felix won't let him.

I'm outside, facing the sky, and letting the drizzle cool me off when I finally let go of the external energy. After catching my breath, I hail a taxicab, knowing that I seriously just dodged a bullet.

EIGHT

I n the morning, something's different. I blink the sleepiness out of my eyes. I never pull my curtains. I need the clay, brick, cement, and glass structures. The anticipation of seeing my inanimate friends is the reason I open my eyes every morning at seven. But all I see is thick fog rubbing against the tall glass walls. With amazement, I scoot to the edge of the bed. I cannot believe this. I've never seen anything like it in New York City, only in Cambridge, and only on that late afternoon when I first came in contact with Baron Ford.

As I drag to the bathroom, I debate whether to call in with an excuse to stay home. I'm dreading the foggy walk to the office and facing Michael. I'm uncomfortable with lying, though. I don't do it and never have. As I spread toothpaste on my electric toothbrush, I think about how easy it would be to just say an emergency family situation came up and I can't elaborate because it's private.

I wrap my hair in my usual bun while trying to talk myself into being brave enough to tell the truth, just not the whole truth.

I'll say, "Michael, sorry, I had to leave."

He'll ask, "Why?"

I can't say because I thought I'd never see Baron Ford ever again. The guy who showed me the night of my life and then, *poof*, vanished.

I'll just say, "Because I wasn't feeling too well— a bit nauseous, actually." That's the truth.

As I slip into my black skirt, the telephone rings. I want to let it go straight to voicemail, but I have a feeling I know who it is. So I rush to answer it, planning on making it quick.

"Hello," I say.

"Clarity?"

Just as I thought. It's Freda. "Mom, I'll call you later."

"Is there fog outside?" she asks.

"What?"

"Is there fog outside or not?" she snaps.

I'm still confused and wondering if she's drunk. I assume she's calling to whine about how the fog has ruined her New York shopping spree trip. I think she's supposed to be in town later this after- noon or by early evening. I'd almost forgotten that we're supposed to have dinner tomorrow.

"Clarity!"

"What?" I stop hopping around, trying to put on the second shoe.

"Do you see fog?"

I look outside. "Yes."

"Did you go anywhere last night?"

"Yes, why?"

She's quiet for a few moments. "Where?"

I sense the seriousness in her tone. It's quite alarming. "I attended an event after work, but I didn't stay long. Why do you want to know?"

"I see. Did you run into any old friends?"

My head flinches back. "Old friends? Mom, are you okay?"

"Did you?"

"Like who?"

She hesitates. "Just answer the question, Clarity."

A picture of Baron flickers in my mind. "No." We didn't run into each other so that was not a lie.

I sense the tension in her silence. I wish she were here so I could attempt to get a read on her. It's hard to use my ability on Freda. I've never discussed this *thing* I have with her, and yet I feel that she knows I have it. Only because I've always suspected that she controls what I'm able to pull from her.

"Mom, I'm fine," I say. I already feel as though I'm running late. "I'll call you later."

"Do *not* leave the apartment," she orders.

"What?" It sounds as though we're back at square one. I want to just go ahead and ask if she was out last night drinking.

My cell phone goes dead. I stand there for a moment, pondering Freda's instructions. She must be off her rocker if she thinks I'm going to un-plan my day to host her last-minute visit that may not happen because of the fog. I'm positive that's the reason she called. All the tension in her voice was about—*her*. Moving forward with my plans for my day just might destroy the plans she has for *our* day.

Just like that, I'm mad at my mother. I stomp over to my closet and take out a red-and-yellow floral-print silk blouse, slip it on, button it up, stuff the hem into my black pencil skirt, and wrap up in a warm cashmere trench coat. I check my phone for bars, but there aren't any. *Oh well, I guess I won't be hearing from Freda any time soon.* With no time to spare, I rush out the door.

CHAPTER
NINE

Outside, the fog is so thick I can barely see my hand in front of my face. I hear sirens and tires screeching, voices cursing, horns honking. That's the normal chorus of the morning, but the symphony is playing a louder, more violent tune.

I can walk from home to work with my eyes closed, though. There's no danger of me turning down the wrong corner and heading down the wrong street. The fog isn't stopping me from sensing the world around me. I hear my heels tap the ground like they usually do. A bus rolls by with extra caution. The regular foot traffic passes me. Energies are fleeting. This morning, I feel one energy follow me for four blocks.

Normally, I would ignore that. Sometimes we city dwellers find ourselves on the same path, strangers heading to the same place. But I must admit that I'm alarmed. I know it's a male, and his attention is trained on me.

I check over my shoulder and see bodies breaking through the vapors to stand beside or behind me. None of their energies is that of my predator. I could jaywalk, but traffic is crazy. Headlights flash, horns blast, tires screech, and voices curse. However, the greater part of traffic is at a standstill, rolling an inch a minute. No one is prepared for this. Behind me, two women discuss it.

The first says, "On the news this morning, they said they don't know where it came from."

The second lady says, "You think it's…?"

"What?"

"Toxic gas or something?"

"We're all alive. I feel fine, but who knows how I'll feel next week."

Now everyone in earshot is anxious. They're all thinking maybe they should go home and make sure the windows are sealed and follow this phenomenon on the news. Maybe Freda knows something I don't, but it's too late for me to turn back. Plus the eerie presence following me has disappeared. All I have to do is cross the street and I'll be near the office, so I move forward. A few people branch off, choosing to return home.

The lobby of the building is not nearly as crowded as usual. There isn't a line at the café, so I walk right in to buy my breakfast sandwich and coffee. The elevator going up isn't crowded this morning. At the agency, those who decided to show up are anxious. Attendance seems low. Even Barbara called in sick. I heard the panic in her voice in her message. I'm almost praying that panic kept Michael at home too.

The instant messenger on my screen beeps. *You're in—good. Come see us?*

I sit and wonder who "us" are. I need a moment with the city view, but of course there's no view. I stare out into the white. In a few seconds, I'll have to get up and take that walk to face judgment. After taking a few deep breaths, the strangest thing happens. A huge black butterfly with white spots lands on the glass, right in front of my face. I study every centimeter of the insect. I can even see its beady little eyes. They're looking back at me.

Get out now. I will protect you.

I hear that as plain as day in my head. That's insane, of course. What's even more cuckoo is that

I'm sure it's coming from the butterfly. I turn away from the thing and study my office. The desk. The computer. The sofa. The papers. I need to be reminded that I live in the real world, a universe where butterflies have no thoughts.

No part of me is settled when I decide to drink half of my cup of coffee for courage, and I head off to meet whoever "us" are in Michael's office. I know it's not who I dread the most—Baron Ford. I don't feel his energy, but I never could. I'm trying to get a sense before I get there, but I come up empty. Even Michael's energy eludes me. I see that as a blessing.

If my ability goes away, I'll be a happier person. I'd be free. I could live my life without fear. I know this is why I stick so close to my parents, because they're two out of the three people in the world who know I'm different. Aries knows, but I haven't seen her in years. I've allowed Felix and Freda to rule every decision of my life. Felix even chose Harvard University for me. He just told me where to report, and there I went. I can't help but feel my parents' strange protection all the time. Strange, because they've been absent all of my life. I can't remember ever having a discussion that lasted more than thirty minutes with either of them. Even when shopping with Freda, she's on her cell phone most of the time, with her agent or producer or some friend who's just as shallow as she is. Felix likes to get to the nitty-gritty of why we're meeting and be done with it.

If my ability is gone, I'll tell Michael to take this job and shove it, and then I'll tell him to relay that message to the partners and to my father. I'll pack up my office, walk out, and go somewhere and probably teach. Art. Or English. Maybe math. I'll teach whatever I can. High school students. Maybe college. Even better, fifth-graders.

I've never felt myself smiling this broadly when I walk up to Leona's desk. "Good morning, Leona."

I can't feel or be who she is at the moment. I do see her brows furrow, questioning my mood. I don't think she's ever seen me smile this big before. I don't smile much. I'm not a happy person.

"Hi," she says tentatively.

I don't think she knows what to say next. Maybe she does. I don't know because I can't embody her! I smile broader. "Is Michael inside?"

"Um, yes. He's waiting for you."

"Thanks." I'm still a grinning fool.

She smiles too. "You're welcome."

I'm riding high. Head lifted to the sky. Back

straight. Contemplating freedom. Until I open the door, and my heart sinks to my toes. I think the joints in my legs will lose all their strength and allow me to collapse on the gray-flecked, industrial carpet.

"Good morning, Miss Parker."

My tongue is locked, lips stuck in an O shape.

"Or is it Missus?" he amends. *Baron Ford amends.*

"Just call me Clarity," I struggle to say and walk over to shake his hand. I pull back quickly.

His hand is ice cold. I remember how warm he felt so long ago. He doesn't look so well, either. He's deathly white, and his sea-blue eyes seem a cruddy cement color. There's no life in them, and they make me shiver.

"Have a seat, Clarity." Michael shoves his hand toward the empty seat beside Baron Ford. "And it's Miss. You're not married, right, Clarity?"

It sounds as though he thinks my marital status is an advantage for the discussion we're about to have. "No," I answer with caution. I find the strength to move to the seat beside Baron.

Clarity…

I hear this in my head. I look out the window of Michael's office, and there's the butterfly again. Just like every other New Yorker today, I'm on the verge of panicking. Not because of the fog but because insects are talking to me.

Clarity.

This time, it isn't the butterfly. I recognize who called my name without opening his mouth; it is Baron Ford!

"I've been running some ideas with Mr. Ford, but he wanted to hear what you had for him too," Michael says.

"Missed you last night," Baron actually says with that smirk. Even though his ambiance is dull, that smirk lights him up like the Christmas tree at Rockefeller Center.

"Um," I start with a stumble, "sorry about that." I cut my eyes toward Michael. "I became achy all of sudden and thought it would be best to leave." I look at Baron again. "But I was definitely going to call you and schedule a meeting."

And there went my first lie ever.

"Fine," Michael says dismissively.

That's what I like about Michael. He knows how to forget about the past and get on with the future. He's a staunch believer in no harm, no foul. He's a good man but consumed by work. I met his wife once. She's a beautiful, lonely woman. She's smart but fears he doesn't treat her that way. As she shook my hand, she was trying to figure out why she loves him. Other women just wonder if he's screwing me.

"You've read the media objectives I sent over yesterday, right?" Michael asks me.

"Yes," I said after clearing my throat.

"Then what are your thoughts on creative approaches?"

What's strange is that I still can't get a read on Michael. The butterfly hasn't flown away—it's watching Baron Ford and me.

"Well," I start, "your company is virtually new—"

"Wait," Baron interrupts.

He's got my and Michael's confused attention.

"Clarity, would you mind if we discuss this over a cup of coffee?" He stands, which tells me that he's not really asking; he's telling me.

"Sure," Michael answers for me and stands too.

I rise to my feet. "Okay, sure."

"Thank you." Baron bows graciously. "After you."

I start toward the door but stop and turn to look at Michael, who hasn't budged. "Are you coming?"

The butterfly goes crazy behind the window. *No,*

don't go, it says. I glance at Baron, who's also staring at the butterfly.

I'm not going to hurt her, he tells it.

Then the butterfly calls him, *Cursed one by evil. You are not allowed here.*

I look at Baron, who remains calm after being cursed by a butterfly. "Cursed one by evil?" What the hell did the insect mean by that?

Baron stands and then opens Michael's door. "Good, coffee then. After you, Clarity?"

The way he looks at me still makes my thighs quiver.

I rise to my feet. One last look at the butterfly, I tell Michael we'll pow-wow later and then walk out of his office. For sure, I've officially lost it.

TEN

Baron and I ride silently down the elevator. We have the matter of the talking butterfly to discuss but unfortunately we're not alone. Two other people are riding with us. When we get to the café, there's not a soul present, not even behind the counter. We sit at a small round table in the back. The fog still hugs the glass walls. I look for the butterfly, but it's not there.

I lean across the table. "What are you doing here?"

He studies me with his gorgeous lips parted, although they're bluish, like they're drained of blood. Actually, his whole face looks drained of blood. "Do you know who you are yet?" he finally asks.

"Yes," I say. I'm really not in the mood for his strange questions. "I'm Clarity Parker, and you just paid the company I work for an insane amount of money to be involved with me, I guess. I want to know why."

"I can't get near you anywhere but here. There's no protection here."

"What?" He sounds insane.

"She hasn't told you anything, has she?" he asks.

"Who's she?"

"Your guardian."

"My guardian? Could you for once make sense?"

"The woman at the apartment that night," he says, remaining calm.

"You mean my mother?"

"Is that what she's calling herself? She's definitely not your mother."

My stomach feels as if it takes a dive to my toes as I ponder what he just revealed. I recall that strange night when he and Freda came face to face. I thought I'd seen her eyes flash yellow, but I blamed it on fatigue. However, there are a million other things about Freda that have always made me question whether or not we're related. We look nothing alike. Although I do resemble my father.

"She is too my mother," I weakly counter. If she isn't, then I'll be too upset to live on.

"Listen,"—he leans in very close to me—"I'm forbidden to tell you who you are. But she's not. I'm forbidden to tell you who I am, but she's not." He sits up straight again. "I want to tell you, Clarity. Because…I love you."

"You love me?" I whisper.

He takes my hands and I let him. "Too much."

"But you don't know me."

Suddenly, he squeezes both sides of his head and groans. I push back in my seat because strangely, I feel his deep pain. It hurts more than anything I've ever felt. It's as if a boulder knocked me in the head and didn't kill me, so now I must endure the agony. As he shoots to his feet, I try to release his energy, but I'm unable to. I think he knows I'm experiencing his torture.

He squeals, "We'll meet soon, Clarity," and rushes out of the café.

I sit here alone, staring dejectedly at my hands. The pain in my head has subsided. On impulse, I turn to look out the window. The fog has lifted. Every inch of it. It's a clear, dank day. I look toward the counter, and two girls in black, tight T-shirts ring up the orders of the first two—now three—

customers who've walked into the café. It's as if the life button has been pushed, and everything is back to normal.

ELEVEN

I'm working late into the night. The desk lamp beside my computer is the only source of light in my office. My shoulders ache; the back of my neck is tight. Even though I massage my temples, my head still throbs. If I could go to sleep right here and be comfortable, I would. I feel this way often. Something tells me it's my diet. I feel best on days I don't eat a breakfast sandwich or drink coffee. I think it's time to erase both from my diet.

Today was a long day of meetings, planned and impromptu. I felt pulled in every direction, forced to concentrate on everything from brand contacts to media strategies, target audiences, and communication goals. Then there was a debriefing on four campaigns we marked up. I truly want to know why I do this for a living and why I'm returning in approximately ten more hours to continue working at a job I loathe. But finally, it's time to pack it up and officially end this workday, and that's what I do.

With all that went on after my encounter with Baron, he's still at the forefront of my mind. Why would he say Freda isn't my mother? I want to accuse him of playing a sick game, but I can't. As my computer powers down, I call Freda. Of course I get her answering service. After the beep, I don't know what to say. I want to ask, "Mom, I mean, Freda, are you my mother?" Or maybe, "Mom, I mean, Freda, what in the world is a guardian and why do I need one?"

Instead I say, "Um, could you give me a call when you get a chance? There's something I want to talk to you about."

At a few minutes past eight, I switch off the desk lamp and walk out of the office. The floor is buzzing with activity. All those who chose to stay home earlier due to the fog are in playing catch-up. All hands are on deck for Red Yard. Everyone is so stressed out and exhausted that nobody notices me enter the elevator.

I still feel a tiny bit unhinged. My senses are

wide open, and I'm consuming every bit of energy I can as I step into the night. Cabs pass, and I contemplate waving one down. The night lights draw me in like a moth to a flame, and not even fear of unknown danger the butterfly warned me of can convince me not to walk amongst the giants that line the streets. The Chrysler Building, with its pointy head, infuses me with bravery. Up Lexington Avenue I go. Buses swoosh by. Cars swoosh by. It's cocktail hour, so sidewalks are buzzing with people entering and exiting bars, restaurants, and lounges. I just want to go home.

When I turn down 67th, heading toward First, I feel it again. *That presence is back.* I train my eyes on Beekman Theater. There's an event tonight, so the courtyard is filled with a very hip, posh crowd. I take comfort in the human company as I speed up and pass them. I trot a little because whoever is following me is gaining ground. I glance over my shoulder before making it to the corner of 2nd Avenue.

Traffic's dense so I have to wait for the walk signal to turn green. I turn back to see who's behind me. Then, I spot him—a man I've never seen before. All I can see are the whites of his eyes, and his pale face wears a tense expression. He's dead set on his goal, and that is to destroy me. My heart pumps blood at the speed of light.

There's a break in traffic, and even though the red sign is telling me to Don't Walk, I go anyway. An oncoming yellow cab barely misses me with a series of blasts of its horn. I look behind me. I sigh with relief. He didn't make it. A slow passing bus gives me time to duck into a narrow alley.

My back hugs the wall as I wait for him to pass. I'm holding my breath, and although I want to take in more oxygen, I can't. He's getting closer and realizes I'm no longer visible. He's a clever man, this fellow who's following me. He stops, takes inventory of our surroundings. He's asking himself where I could have gone.

I shut my eyes tighter because he's right upon me. Then, I feel a blade against my throat and his arm against my chest, pinning me to the cement wall, I know I'm trapped like a rat in a corner. *This is how I'll die.* I look deep into those cold, dead eyes of his. It's like he sees me, but he doesn't.

"Why?" I manage to whisper.

"I can't," he whimpers.

The first expression I see from him is agony. I hear in his head two voices telling him to do it, a woman and man I don't recognize.

You do what I say. Now kill her. Spill her precious blood, the crazed woman says.

The edge of the blade has already dug into my skin. I feel the intense sting as droplets of blood trickle down my neck. A young woman murdered in a New York City alley—what a cliché.

When I close my eyes to let go of the assassin's energy and welcome death, a wall of wind hits us. I'm knocked to the pavement, and I open my eyes. I'm in a cloud of blinding white light. There are two energies with me: one is an unconscious life force and the other is like music—a hymn— soprano and sung by an angelic choir. I touch my neck to feel the shallow slice on my throat. The stranger must've killed me, and this is heaven or hell. *Someone with my ability must be made of something that's not good.*

I blink, and it's dark again with only the lights from the main street stabbing into the crevice. I stumble to my feet. I'm alive, because the tiny line cut into my neck still stings. If I were dead, wouldn't I not feel pain?

"Clarity, are you okay?"

I spin around to see Baron Ford standing at the entrance of the fissure. His face is tense, as if he's distressed.

"I think so," I say, taking stock of my body. I can stand, though my knees are shaking. I can feel my hands, although they're shaking too.

Baron quickly faces the street as if he hears something. "He'll be back."

"Who'll be back?" I'm panicking.

He rushes over to me at a remarkable speed. I have no time to process the logic of him moving so fast because I can't believe Baron Ford is this close to me again.

"I did this to you," he confesses. "Zina found you because of me."

"Who's that? You have to say something that makes sense," I plead.

Baron's entire beautiful face grimaces. Whatever is happening to him is definitely painful. Then his eyes rest on my neck, and the pain appears gone. Suddenly, I can experience what he's feeling. This ability is starting to come and go. He's thirsty, parched. I've never felt such thirstiness from a person in my life. His hand slowly extends toward my neck, but he touches my cheek instead. I close my eyes. He's warm. This morning he was so cold.

"There." He closes his eyes.

I can no longer feel or hear him, and it's not because he's not thinking or feeling. "What's happening?" Can he feel it? The passion between us? The heat his touch has stirred in me? I'm sweating. I want to rip off my clothes to get cool, and I want to rip off my clothes to give myself to him.

I see his face moving closer to mine. In less than a second, our lips should meet. But then the wind that hit me earlier smashes into us again. Just like that, Baron is no longer in front of me. I feel the loss of him. I whip my face around and see two men tussling up ahead. One of them is Baron; the other is a man in black. I cannot see his face.

Baron shouts, "I'm not going to harm her."

The man says nothing, only fights. There's a weapon in his hand—a long, thin, shiny instrument that looks to be on fire. I think it's a sword.

"Command him to stop," Baron shouts.

He eludes the fiery blade as it comes down against the wall and slices through the cement. The man doesn't stop; he takes another swipe at Baron. The scrimmage is unreal. They're moving faster than is humanly possible. I can hardly follow it.

Baron pleads with me again. "Tell him to stop!"

I'm trying to process this. Baron is struggling with a stranger. I'm bewildered. When I see them at a standstill, the sword raised high and Baron's hand clutching the man's arm, I sense Baron's moment of defeat.

"Stop! I command you to stop." I wait to see what happens.

Instantly, the man puts the sword away and faces me. Even in the dark, I see his entire face scowling at me. What's even stranger is that his skin is black and his eyes are ice blue and glowing.

"Think of me," Baron says.

He moves away at a speed that makes me think I'm indeed dead and now *tripping* somehow. I'm left alone with the man in black, who doesn't look happy that I stopped him from slicing off Baron's head.

He snarls. "Why did you do that?" He has an accent, one I've never heard before.

That's the first time I hear any noise from him. I can't hear his thoughts or feel his emotions. He didn't even grunt once during the fight. Though I'm trying, I can't break through and pick up any energy from him.

So I ask, "Am I dead?"

"No." He moves closer to me.

I see his face more clearly now. His skin is the color of brass, and his eyes are actually glowing—blue. Though I can't get a read on him, I figure he's not going to hurt me since I told him to stop his attack on Baron, and he did as I said.

"Who are you?" I ask.

"Go home now. You are safe."

"What do you mean?" I ask.

"Go."

"But—"

"Go."

I realize that's all he has to say to me. I glance over my shoulder at the street. I can't imagine why no one saw us and reported the fighting. Then I remember this is New York City. I sigh. When I turn back to face the stranger, he's gone. Fear makes me run out of the alley and onto the sidewalk to rejoin the real world where men don't move faster than superheroes or wield blades of fire.

TWELVE

I make it to my door and my hand shakes as I put the key into the lock, turn and then open. I gasp as I slap my hand on chest.

"Mom?" Freda is standing at the window, staring out into the night.

"Why didn't you do what I asked?" she asks in a dry tone.

I enter and flick on the lights, wondering why she's standing in the dark. Freda's not the sort of person who finds the dark comforting.

"No," she scolds. "Keep it off."

I do as I'm told. "What's going on? First butterflies are talking to me. Then Baron Ford shows up. And then—"

She whips around. "Baron Ford?"

When I look at her beautiful face, I remember something. "He says you're not my mother. Is that true?"

She walks past me to stand at the door. "Get what you need, and let's go."

I dig my feet into the glistening hardwood, refusing to move until I get answers. "Is it true?" I cross my arms.

"You'll learn everything soon. See that cut on your throat? You escaped this time, but they're not done with you yet. Anyone and everyone is going to be looking to spill your blood."

"What? You're not making sense, Mom."

We stare at each other in the darkness. I can see her thinking, and without saying a word, she tells me to go to the window.

I stop for one reason and one reason only. My entire life, she's never communicated with me in that manner. I assumed she knew about my abilities, but she's never confirmed it.

Yes, I know, she says.

My legs turn to mush. I want to bawl like a baby and hug myself. Aren't mothers supposed to be able to take away such torturous pains? For her to know my agony all of these years and do nothing? Maybe Baron is right. She couldn't be my mother.

I see on her face that she's listened to everything I just thought. I'm not able to look at her any longer, so I do as I'm told and go to the window.

At first, people walk by. As I continue studying the sidewalks and road, I see one person stop, and then another, and another. A crowd gathers in front of my building. They're looking up, right at my window. It's so weird that I step back. I don't want to be seen by them.

"They're looking for you," Freda says.

"Why?" I still have my neck stretched so I can cautiously view them.

These people are just average citizens, about twelve or thirteen of them. Even cars have stopped in the middle of the street.

"They're under the influence of magic, and they want you dead. They can't see you, but they know you're up here. They can't come in because the building is protected."

There goes that *protected* word again. Baron mentioned it this morning. Apparently my place of employment is not protected, but my residence is. In my mind, I hear her tell me to look out again. I do. The crowd has dispersed, and traffic rolls by smoothly.

"I can only hold them off for so long," she says.

I'm very close to being a believer. I nod and move to the bedroom. Freda's right behind me. I drag a suitcase out of the closet.

"Pack light. Just take what's important to you," she says.

I look into her face and then around the room. What's important to me? I have the expensive clothes that the woman standing in the doorway bought me. I wonder if this new Freda will be slighted if I take nothing but the clothes on my back. I pack underwear and a toothbrush and toothpaste. I leave the makeup—I never needed it anyway. I snatch up my purse, look around the room, and think about how sad it is that I have nothing of importance in my life.

"I'm ready," I say.

Freda watches me with a frown and glassy eyes. Did she just hear me contemplate the things of importance?

"I'm sorry," she says.

"About what?" I ask, playing dumb.

"About not being able to be more to you. I knew, *we* knew, this day would come."

"When you say *we*, do you mean Felix too?"

She lifts her eyebrows. "You'll learn more later. There's no time for conversation."

"But are you my mother?" I ask in a timid voice.

The answer is easy enough: yes or no.

Although half of me doesn't want to know the truth, half of me does. I halfway don't want her to be my mother, but for the sake of not being deceived all of these years, I halfway do.

"Biologically, no," she answers.

I want to faint.

"Let's get out of here now," she says, warning me that we have no time for my reaction.

Again, I nod and follow her out into the hallway. The lights are dim, and neighbors stand in their doorways watching us. The scene gives me the creeps.

She picks up the pace and so do I.

"Why are they watching us?" I ask.

"They're not giving up."

"Who?"

"Your friend Baron and others like him."

I shake my head. "No, not Baron. He'd never put me through this."

We make it to the elevator and ride down. The lights flicker.

"You stay away from him," Freda warns.

"I don't think he's trying to hurt me."

"It's in his nature to hurt you. He won't be able to help himself, Clarity. And it doesn't matter anyway. If he's with you, they'll find you. So stay away from him."

We make it to the lobby and the double doors slide open. A black Town Car with tinted windows is parked in front of the building. Freda runs up to it and swings open the back passenger door.

"Get in," she commands.

I slide all the way over to give her space to enter. But she shuts me in, and before I can respond, the car shoots away from the curb. I twist around to glare at her out the back window. She stands there, watching me disappear. When she's out of sight, I flip around in my seat, still confused. I can't believe that's it. She puts me in the car and watches me leave, and that's it. I wonder if I'll ever see her again. What about Felix? Will I ever see him again?

THIRTEEN

After a full day like today, I'm truly exhausted. My eyes want to close, but my brain is active. The stranger, the one who saved me earlier, is driving.

He's going fast, cutting in and out of traffic. The lights all cut to green, giving him free passage. I've never maneuvered out of the city so fast. In minutes, he's racing down George Washington Bridge. He doesn't even stop to pay the toll. The lights that run across the bridge pass us in a blur. I wonder if we're even visible, because this stranger cuts in and out of traffic, but no one honks at him. No one in New York gets away with how he's driving.

I hadn't realized it, but my fingernails are dug into the seat. I want to ask him to please slow down, but then I remember the strange scene on the sidewalk and in the hallway. Maybe for some weird reason—truly, this is all weird—he can't slow down. Instead of complaining, I close my eyes and think about the better parts of the day, which are all the moments spent with Baron Ford.

He and I almost kissed. I want that kiss. I've read books about stuff like this. A mysterious, dangerous stranger falls in love with a hapless girl, and the guy turns out to be something ridiculous, like a vampire. I can't help but chuckle out loud at that. When I open my eyes, the strange man is looking at me through the rearview mirror. I close my eyes again and go back to more satisfying thoughts.

When Baron touched me this morning, his hand was cold. He looked so sallow, I thought he'd fall over and die. Why does being with him make me feel so alive, even when he looked so dead?

We haven't known each other long at all. We had days in the lounge when he didn't say a word to me. Then the night he showed up at my doorstep, we went to the gallery and spent the rest of the night bathing in each other's warmth. The warmth…it's like soaking in a hot tub, frolicking in the warm waters of a natural hot springs. When our lips connected, that heat dug deep into my heart. I swear, I think I can love Baron Ford, the peculiar guy with an ancient beauty, forever.

When I open my eyes again, there's a hint of daylight in the cloudy sky. I'm curled up with my right cheek smashed against the top of the black leather seat. By the way my neck aches, I must've fallen asleep and been out for a while. I yawn, stretch, and look at the eyes that are watching me through the rearview mirror.

"Where are we going?" I ask. I try to butter him up with a smile, but he just puts his eyes back on the road. I shake my head. "Really? You're not going to tell me?"

Still, he says nothing. I'm not prepared to give up, but the landscape catches my attention. Cinnamon-red leaves flutter in a constant wind. The hue runs deep into the terrain, hovering on both sides of the road and casting a gray shadow over the car. It's an enchanted scene, a different beauty than the rising buildings with their many windows. I see a mixture of yellow, orange, and red leaves. The brisk breeze even makes the fallen ones dance across the road. It's gorgeous.

"I'm sorry, whatever your name is," I say, remembering my current situation, "but you have to give me something. Maybe we can start with your name? Then you can tell me where we're going? That's if you can talk. You can still talk, can't you? I've heard you speak before."

I think I'm waiting for an answer but not really expecting one. All I hear is the smooth hum of the engine and the car moving at a very fast speed.

But then he unexpectedly says, "I talk."

My mind hangs on his two words. His voice is deep and lacks something I cannot quite define. But I want to keep him talking.

"Can you tell me your name?" I ask with a hint of caution. I learned a long time ago to meet people where they are.

"Viesel Egos."

"Viesel Egos, where are we going?"

I watch his thin brown lips twitch. My carefully crafted question makes him consider past the script he's performing for me. The great thing about spending years with my ability is that I have learned to read people without hearing or being them.

I lift an eyebrow. "So you're not going to tell me?"

"I am not," he says.

I pause to let it sink in that he's actually serious.

"All right, then." I nestle deeper and touch the fresh wound on my neck, and something tells me I'm in deep trouble. But I'm not ready to stop learning all I can from my untalkative companion.

"Viesel Egos," I say and wait for a quarter of his upper face to appear in the rearview mirror. "Why did you stop when I asked you to in the alley?"

His face disappears from the mirror as he chooses not to answer.

"Can I tell you what to do?"

Still he says nothing.

I need to test my hypothesis. "Stop the car," I say in a low, unsure voice.

I don't have to wait long until the car veers to the side of the road and comes to a halt. I'm stunned into silence, allowing what just happened to sink in. Is he screwing around with me? I'm certain he's not. I've already concluded that Viesel Egos is a serious person. He stares at the empty road ahead without uttering a word.

I take stock of what's going on inside me. I feel

ashamed that I made this man stop for no reason other than to test my power over him. Mom, I mean, Freda, would not be happy with me right now.

Never assert your power because you can, only if you truly need to.

I remember her repeating that to me when I was very young, and it has always stuck with me. A lot of what I believe came from some pivotal years when I can't remember what I did or said to spark those lessons.

"Sorry." I drop my face to hide my shame. "Please continue on."

Viesel cuts the engine back on, and we move forward again. I'm still too embarrassed to look at the back of his bald head. I nestle against the door and stare out the window.

"Where I'm taking you is the only place you'll be safe," he says out of the blue.

In the quiet that remains after he speaks for the first time without my prompting, I say, "Thank you, Viesel Egos."

Although he doesn't say *you're welcome*, I can feel his gracious reply in the silence.

I close my eyes to fantasize about Baron Ford again. There's something comforting about interacting with him in my imagination. We're in the alley, and he does kiss me this time. I pull from memories from our first kiss in Cambridge five years ago. My mind goes deeper into imagining us together. What if I had stayed at the Red Yard event that night? What if Baron had joined me and the boys in our discussion and I laid out the perfect media contact plan for him? What if he liked it so much he wanted to toast to it right then? He and I ease into a dark corner. He asks if I'm married now.

I say, "Not even close."

He tells me he isn't either because he's never gotten over me.

I ask, "What happened? Why did you go away, never to be heard from until now?"

It takes him a long while to come up with an excuse I'll accept, but I go with the story about how a death in the family called him back to that small, unimportant place he fled from. Not until now had he the will to take life by the horns and go after everything he wants, including me.

Then he asks me, "Now that we're back in each other's lives, what next?"

That's when I open my eyes and realize I must've been dreaming during a catnap. But even with my eyes open, the question the man in my dreams asked still hangs in my mind. *What next?* I don't know.

We're driving through a dark, dense forest. I twist my neck to see around the driver's seat and out the front window. The muddy road we're cutting through is narrow, and it seems Viesel Egos has picked up even more speed. I see him checking all the mirrors as he goes. It's easy to sense his alarm.

"Stay down in your seat," he orders.

I nod and do as I'm told. It's not long before I see something threatening. A force runs alongside us, bending the trees about ten layers deep into the brush. Instinctively, I tune in to it, pulling in its energy. A piercing sound, like iron fingernails scratching downward on a chalkboard, goes off in my head. I scream and smash both of my palms against my ears.

"Think of nothing," Viesel Egos shouts as he cuts a sharp right.

I close my eyes to empty my thoughts. I force myself to focus on the black I see behind my eyelids. The car zooms full speed ahead, and I dare not open my eyes. If I look, I'll lose the concentration I'm forcing myself to maintain.

Then I'm hit by an extremely bright light I see

even behind my closed eyelids. The car slows down. I feel as if the threat is gone, so I open my eyes to see that we've stopped in the middle of a muddy road. The trees hover over us, but none of them are bending. Somehow we evaded the frightening force that appeared to be chasing us.

FOURTEEN

It's calm here. The sky is a cloudless, perfect royal blue. The leaves are deep green, and without my asking, Viesel Egos rolls down the back windows. I feel the soft breeze caress my face. The temperature is perfect. I've felt evenings like this in California, but they usually showed up after a long, hot day that had been tempered by ocean breezes.

Viesel Egos moves out of the driver's seat at the same time the door beside me automatically opens. "You're here."

I grab my skimpy bag and purse and step out into the illusory day. The direct sun falls like a warm whisper on my face, and I can't help but remember the kiss Baron and I almost shared last night. I wonder if I'll ever stop living in regret that it didn't happen.

"There," Viesel Egos says and nods toward the top of a stairway made of white sandstone.

"Okay," I mutter.

My steps are unsure, and when I get there, my hand slides up and down the soft rail. It's so smooth, so white; it looks as if the elements have never battered it.

"Do I go down?" I ask Viesel Egos.

There's no reply. I turn to look at him. Not only is he gone, but the car is gone too. I waste no time trotting down the stairs, trying to leave the forest as far behind me as I can. When I feel I've journeyed far enough down, I turn to look behind me and see nothing but stark white light. The rays momentarily stun my eyes. I blink and continue on. I feel as though I'm a solid five minutes in, and I'm still skipping down the steps. The stairway has curled a number of times, and I finally see a bottom in sight.

I have one more pillow of bright light to walk through before I stand under a thick canopy of leaves. The trees catch my eyes because they're a species I never thought could exist. The trunks are perfect circles, maybe five feet in circumference, and have deep ridges cut into the wood every six inches or so. Their surface is made of smooth, bright blue granular particles that run deep into the crevices. The trees look so natural, as if they haven't been designed or cut. The deep green leaves are flat and shaped liked six-pointed stars. I look at the ground because I'm just realizing how mushy it is. Under my feet lies grass so green and so plush that it looks fake.

Clarity, a woman's voice whispers in my head.

I look around. I see not a soul in this meadow of perfectly spaced trees. How unreal is this? I must be dead or something. Although I should be afraid, I'm not. I let my feet guide me and my instincts carry me. I actually feel as if I'm walking on marshmallows. Maybe this is heaven. I've been a good girl all of my life. I couldn't help it—there are rules written in my brain and heart that I can't defy. Could this be my forever reward? If so, I can completely accept it.

When I reach a glassy stream, I slip off my shoes, pick them up, and walk across the tepid water. I could swim in it, bathe in it—drink from it. Instead I keep moving, very much aware that I'm very hungry and still wearing the skirt and blouse I wore to the office yesterday. Also, my head hurts. To stop the ache, I pull my hair out of its bun and let it fall free. Then I realize my feet aren't wet, and I slip my shoes back on.

"This place is Enu," the woman says, but this time I hear an actual voice.

I spin around and face the most beautiful creature I think I've ever laid eyes on.

"That's the answer to the question you are asking," she says.

"Right," I barely say, enthralled by her. Her skin is the actual color of soft brown maple wood, and her eyes are pure emerald green. Her hair looks just like mine. It's strange, but I think we favor each other.

"What am I doing here?" I ask.

"You're here because you've been discovered before our time."

"Our time?"

"The time of the daughters, who hold the blood of life."

"Okay…" I say, questioning my sanity. It seems I've walked into the second chapter of a cliché.

"You believe you are insane." She smiles. "No, you believe I am insane!"

"I think we're both crazy. I'm ready to wake up out of this…" I want to say nightmare, but then I remember my interactions with Baron.

Her hand clamps down on my wrist, and she pulls me along. "Let's move along. We must get started."

I see the picture of what brought this urgency on in her mind, and I stop walking. "Wait. What and who is Baron Ford? Where did Viesel Egos go?" I stop myself at two questions.

Her cool demeanor is not even close to matching my frazzled one. "Aren't you hungry?"

I look down at my stomach; it does ache from the lack of food. "I guess I am."

"We'll get you food to eat. I promise to tell you all that I can then."

I believe her. I believe everything about her. Her soul is the purest I've ever sensed. So I nod, and when she smiles, I'm taken aback by how her entire face lights up. Her teeth are pure white, as though she's never drunk a sip of coffee, tea, or red wine. I notice she's wearing a lightweight, sleeveless white cotton dress, and she's barefoot too.

"Can I ask you what your name is?"

"Adore."

I chuckle. "Sounds like Clarity."

She smiles. "It does, doesn't it?"

We laugh together. I want to take my shoes off and walk barefoot like Adore.

Do it.

Grinning, I slip one sixteen-hundred-dollar shoe off and then the other.

Leave them here, she tells me. *They'll find you, if you ever need them.*

If I ever need them? I wonder what that means, but I'm too enthralled by what I'm experiencing to ask. I drop my shoes on the grass. I look back at the black, two-and-a-half-inch-heeled Mary Janes that I'm so used to walking in, I could run a marathon in them and probably win. There's something ceremonious about letting go of them, and I want to rip off my tailored skirt and blouse too.

We're moving so fast across the grass, it almost feels like sprinting. I'm surprised when we come to an abrupt stop at the edge of a cliff. The green grass curves over and runs down the crag at a one-hundred-fifty-foot straight drop. What's even more magnificent is the valley below. Glistening streams cut through the grass and circle quaint garden cottages.

I'm so far up that I can't fully take in the scene below. There are more trees—even my favorites, like weeping willows, sycamores, elms, sugar maples, and so many varieties of oak. The energy emanating from below is the most inviting ever. My heart feels as if it's floating, and my feet are light. I look down at them because it doesn't even feel as though I'm standing anymore.

"This is Enu," Adore says with a smile.

"Hope," I say.

"Yes, Enu is hope."

"It's beautiful. And so…expansive."

Adore takes my right hand into her left. I'm not a touchy-feely person. Normally my hand would tense when touched by someone I'm not romantic with, but her hand feels like an extension of my limb, similar to her soul. When I look at her, I see the black and white butterfly sitting on her left shoulder.

"Wek," she says.

She's come home, it says and then flies off.

"Okay, did a butterfly just talk to you?" I ask, still thinking I'm on a drug-induced trip.

"What's a butterfly?" Her brows are crimped, indicating that was a genuine question.

"The insect that was just on your shoulder," I say.

"Insect? That's a Wek, a watcher of the realm called Earth. He's kept you safe from the moment you breathed the earth's air."

I'm thinking a million things at once.

"Are you ready?" Adore asks, interrupting my thought process. She tightens her grip on my hand and looks straight ahead, out over the steep edge.

"Are we going that way?" I ask, alarmed.

"Yes."

"That drop will flat-out kill me dead."

She giggles. "No, it will not."

"Really?" I'm shocked that it won't. "So is this place like Neverland or something?"

"Neverland? I'm not familiar with that universe."

Then it hits me: she wouldn't know anything about a tale of a boy who never wanted to grow up. They must all love to grow up here in Enu.

"It's not an actual place," I say. "It's from a work of fiction. Not real."

She looks at me with a smile. She's not even giving it a second thought, which is amazing— conversations are usually residual. Adore has great control of her mind.

"Know that nothing can hurt you here. Just move forward. See…"

Adore still has my hand, and the lukewarm air, as fresh as a baby's breath, whisks across my face as we run down the cliff. Our speed is remarkable, matching that displayed by Baron and Viesel during their tussle. At first my stomach drops, tickling my insides, and my head spins as the wind flows up my nose. I feel the rush of pure oxygen. Then it's over. We're at the bottom. It's like the laws of gravity don't apply in this universe called Enu.

One of the unmarked cottages is a little café that holds small round limestone tables and chairs. Even the counters, floors, and walls are made of white limestone. Unlike the cities I've fallen in love with over the years, tall, wide windows are not relished here. There's a cozy feeling that, strangely, makes me feel safe.

Adore and I are the only two patrons. We sit at a table in the middle of the room where a platter of fruit that resembles blueberries and raspberries, plus fresh-baked flat, round rolls and white cream are already set on a table. There's also a tea urn and two cups filled with liquid that smells so delicious my mouth is watering.

"Goshem tea," she says as I look down to study the dark purple substance.

The aroma reaches my nose, and it smells of grapes and mint. It's not coffee. I don't even need the caffeine to pick me up, which is something new for my body. I eagerly take a sip. The taste is out-of-this-world unreal.

"Baron," she says, making sure I'm looking into her eyes. "He's parched."

"Right now?" I'm confused. Why is she telling me Baron's parched, and how does she know that?

"Yes, all the time. He's always thirsty. On the earth, you call them strigoi?"

"Strigoi?"

"Vrykolakas?"

I shake my head. It still doesn't ring a bell.

"How about vampyre?"

Now that makes sense, and my tongue is in my throat. My eyes shoot around the room as if I'm hoping no one heard her.

"Vampires don't exist. That's folklore, fairy-tales," I whisper. Of course no one is around, but it's too embarrassing if even the air hears me discussing the possibility of the existence of vampires.

"Yes, you are correct," Adore says. "Not in the way that they are portrayed. They do thirst for blood, but they can't drink without the free will and knowledge of the sacrifice. It's an eternal thirst for blood, and the vampire is parched until a human sacrifices him- or herself to cure the thirst."

"So you're saying that Baron wants to drink blood?" The world stops, and my brain works overtime. I thought vampires were cold. Why is he so warm to me?

"Because you have the blood of life," she answers after reading my mind again.

"I don't get it." I'm stunned, but I still can't stop eating the sweet berries, cream, and bread set before me. The berries are the perfect ripeness and plumpness. Their juices burst in my mouth and fill my stomach. My limbs feel more invigorated with each bite.

"You'll know everything soon. Finish eating and drinking. We have nothing but time."

When the meal is over, we walk across Enu and pass a male with the smoothest purplish skin. Even more extraordinary is he has actual almond-cut, orange-colored eyes.

Oh, Adore. Oh, Clarity, he says in our minds with a slight bow and the brightest white smile ever.

Who looks like that?

"Oh" is definitely a greeting as Adore answers by saying, *Oh, Tryst*.

Out of common courtesy, I repeat what she says. I glance back at Tryst and wonder where he's going. What do the people of Enu do on a regular day? Their cottages are small but quaint, not glamorous but comfortable. It's a way I've always wanted to live. There are so many trees I could get lost in them. We're walking through a thin forest of trees that hold red, purple, and yellow fruit. Some of the fruit is rectangular-shaped, some even triangular-shaped. It's all so exotic.

"These are trees of life," Adore says, touching one of the yellow, fuzzy-skinned triangular fruit. She pulls it off the tree and hands it to me. "Taste it."

I hesitate but take it and take a bite. It tastes like a fusion of peaches and oranges. I want to explode from delight. I want to merge with the fruit and eat it forever.

"How do you feel?" she asks.

"Like I want to walk on air," I answer, taking another bite.

"This fruit is your fortifier. You eat it, and it gives you life. The more of it you eat, the more of this universe you will become." Adore reaches up, pulls another fruit off the tree, and takes a bite.

Then it strikes me. "So you're saying I'm here to stay?"

"If you go back, they will try to kill you for your blood."

"Who are *they*? Do you mean Baron?"

"Yes." There's a bite to her voice.

I get the feeling she's not too pleased about Baron. I also think she's not elaborating as much as I need her to in order to understand what's going on.

"Look, Adore," I say, quite aware that I just lost my appetite for this fruit, "you say I have blood of life and that makes it dangerous for me to go home. You also said that these people, or creatures or whatever, are supposed to be like vampires—"

"Are vampires," she corrects without a hint of the ridiculous in her tone. She believes what she's told me without doubt, without amusement.

"Okay," I restate, "these vampires can't drink our blood without our free will. I never gave Baron permission to drink my blood." *But that doesn't mean that I wouldn't.* I try to conceal that thought from Adore, but the look on her face—the way her eyes just slightly widen—confirms that she pulled that last thought from my mind anyway.

"You're not a—" She stops short and edits herself. "You're not like everyone else." She continues walking deeper into this forest.

I keep up with her, noticing how the bushels of the trees are thicker now, but the sunlight has not decreased in intensity. The rays touch my skin even through the leaves. Her revelation that I'm not like everyone else doesn't shock me. I've lived in my own skin long enough to know that already.

"But of course you know this already," she says, almost repeating my thoughts verbatim. "Your blood is highly coveted by the Selells, the thirsty, the vampires. Can you imagine being forever thirsty, for blood, but being unable to drink it unless the humans know that if they give of themselves, they will die?"

"What happens when the Selells dies?"

She looks at me for the longest time without saying a word. "I don't know. But when they drink your blood, they live, and you may be damned to the darkness."

I feel a chill overcome me. "What's the darkness?"

"It's eternal damnation."

"But why?" Why do I have to be damned for allowing the man I love his freedom from the thirst? It doesn't seem fair.

"I don't know," Adore admits. She looks at me with a deep curiosity. "But the intensity with which you love Baron Ze Feldis—how does it feel?"

"You mean Baron Ford?"

"He is from the Ze Feldis clan. Born in 1633, on

October 27, your calendar years." She's still waiting for an answer.

"I don't know why I love him this much." I'm sort of shocked by the numbers she just gave me—1633? That's an awfully long time ago.

"Maybe he has enchanted you," she suggests.

Maybe. Maybe not.

She heard that but remains silent as we step out of the forest to face a single cottage encircled by a crystal stream. "This is yours. Come." She moves forward.

I follow. My feet dig deep into the plush grass. I look for a bridge to cross over the water, but I don't see one. I'm about to inquire how we are to get across without getting wet when Adore steps into the stream. I follow her.

"Your Selell has bonded himself to another, and she knows of your existence," Adore offers up out of the blue.

"Do you mean Zina?" I ask.

"Yes, that's what the female is called."

My heart is on the verge of breaking. "What do you mean they're bonded? Is he married to this woman?"

"Selells bond to survive."

"Oh." I recall all the vampire folklore I can

remember. I think that information is out there already. "So he's not married."

She looks confused. "I don't think Selells marry. Only full-blooded humans."

After an awkward moment of silence, I turn to dote on how the door to the cottage sparkles. It opens on its own, and what's inside takes my breath away. The floor is carpeted, and in the middle of the room sits a brown fluffy sofa facing a lit fireplace. The sofa also slightly curves to face a wall-sized window, and what's beyond the glass amazes me. I see my favorite skyscrapers from Manhattan and Cambridge, including the Chrysler Building. Night has fallen over the scene, and what I love so much about a dark metropolis is on display—the lights-off, lights-on effect peppered throughout the terrain.

"Wow" is all I can say.

"It's what you cherish on the earth, is it not?" Adore asks as she steps up next to me. We both stare out the window.

"Is it real?"

"Is it real to you?" she asks.

"I don't know," I say sadly. "I don't know what's real anymore." The only thing that's still real to me is what I feel for Baron.

"First and foremost," she says and waves at the brown fluffy sofa, "sit."

I walk over and take a seat. I love the way my feet feel against the brown and tan shag carpet. Then it hits me; this is the carpet from the residents' lounge at the Bend Condos in Cambridge. Not only the carpet, but the sofa too! We sit and look at each other.

"You must embrace that you are intuitive," she says. "It's your first field of protection. But you have to control it, because they can find you once you open up."

"You're talking about Zina and Baron?"

"No, not the Selells. I mean *the evil.*"

"*The evil?* What's that?" Things are getting even more confusing.

"It's what I said it is—*the evil.*"

I remember the last menacing thing I saw, which was how the trees bent as something unseen pursued us. "Did I see this evil on the way here?

"Yes. It's always looking for a way into Enu."

Again, I picture the violent force bending the trees. It was *so unreal.* Then I remember Viesel Egos and how he told me to clear my thoughts.

"Viesel Egos," I say, "what is he?"

"Egos is neither man nor Enuian. He's made by the hand of the Creator, God himself."

"Wow…that makes sense," I muse. Everything about him was pure perfection. "Is he an angel?"

"No."

"What is he, then?"

"He's your guardian."

"Are you telling me that God created a guardian just for *me*?" That sounds utterly ridiculous. I'm just me, nobody special.

"Yes," she says, "that is correct."

"Oh."

I've spent many nights trying to figure out why I'm equipped to know what people are thinking. Why am I able to get into their skin and walk in their shoes? There hasn't been a hint of an answer until now. I'm too afraid to ask the one question I'm dying to. I've learned enough for today.

Adore rises. Instinctively, I stand too. I know she's about to leave me, and I don't want to be without her. I've never wanted another person around as much as I want Adore. I feel as though I've known her all my life. As though she's part of me and I'm part of her on some mysterious level.

She touches my chin. "You must get some sleep. Your Earth days have been long."

She's right. I'm exhausted. Sharing Adore's aura has kept me energized, but the farther she walks away, the sleepier I get.

"Be-oh, Clarity," she says while moving backward so lightly it's as if she's floating.

I know that *be-oh* is good-bye in Enu, not goodnight. There is no night here. "Be-oh, Adore."

CHAPTER

FIFTEEN

My limbs are light as air when I wake up. My head is more uncluttered than ever. I think I've been asleep for a very long time.

After Adore left, I explored the cottage. The one small bag I packed and my purse were sitting on a shelf inside what looked like a black pearl armoire, along with the Manolo Blahniks I kicked off. I thought I'd lost the bags in the woods, but I guess not.

The bed looked so inviting with its crisp white linens and fluffy pillows. It was some sort of sleigh bed that faced the window so I could sleep watching the buildings. Without delay, my fingers did what I'd wanted them to do all day, which was peel off my skirt, blouse, and underwear. I looked for the bathroom, which was down a short corridor.

The sink, floor, and shower were made of white marble, swirled with lime. I recognized it as the sleek decor of Freda's private bathroom—the one I was forbidden to enter. My lids were heavy. I was sleepier than ever, but it didn't take a genius to figure out that the entire cottage was composed of everything I liked.

After a shower, I slid beneath the covers and went to sleep. My dreams were of Baron Ford. In my dream, we kissed in the dark alley before Viesel Egos showed up.

"I love you, not your blood," he said while pelting my neck with soft, warm kisses.

"Why?" I asked breathlessly, floating from his nearness.

"You're beautiful, sexy, smart, and—unique."

All the lines I'd ever heard from guys who tried to make it with me. All the lines I never believed because, though their mouths spoke those words, their minds and hearts only coveted my body. Over the years, I learned that lust is fleeting.

But with the Baron Ze Feldis of my dreams, I felt him admiring my passion for sketching and sculpting. He thought it was unique that I loved a cityscape so much because of the life it held. When I kissed him in my dream, his defenses were stunned, and I heard him wonder if I'd been made for him. I was on the verge of whispering an answer when he disappeared out of my arms.

I found myself giggling under the sun and chasing the polka-dot butterfly. The warmth of passion I felt for Baron was replaced by the security of Adore next to me. In my dream, it was as if I'd known her all of my life. She was what I never had, and that was a friend. A true friend who felt like family—a sister.

After I woke up, my suit, skirt and blouse, the only clothes I'd brought with me, were gone, and a long cotton spaghetti-strap white dress hung up in the armoire. I slipped it on, happy to have my own Enu outfit, and it fit perfectly.

But now, as I look at the makeshift city beyond my window, complete with moving people, taxicabs, buses, and even smoke from the subway, I hug myself. I don't miss this scene. I do miss what could have been. What if I'd stayed in Manhattan and worked on the Red Yard campaign with Baron Ford, whom I'd had the date of my life with five years ago in Cambridge? We might have started dating regularly. He would ask me more questions about myself, and I would tell him everything.

I never pictured my life with a husband or children. I've been told that it's a beautiful thing, but my fantasy has always been to be free from my ability. Even in Enu, after learning of vampires and an alternative humanoid race, I still want to be free of this ability.

My eyes are closed, and I see myself living the life I always dreamt of—walking into a classroom of children, teaching them all I know about arithmetic and being kind to their peers. I hear a violent slam on the glass wall. When I open my eyes, blood is spattered on the glass, and the word "help" written in it. One blink later, it's gone.

"Are you ready?"

Startled, I turn to look behind me. Adore is there, wearing that electrifying smile of hers. I wonder if she saw the blood and the word *help*, but she gives no indication that she did. I don't want to mention it because of the paradox between who she is and the world on the opposite side of the glass.

When we're outside, I look over the valley. It's just as quaint as it was the day I arrived. The sun wraps around me to give me a warm hug. I notice there are hardly any other living beings out. Actually, none at all. I think about this as we head deeper into the grassland with no trees.

"But you're not an angel, right?" I ask out of the blue.

"Do you mean me?"

"Yes. What are you, Adore?"

She stops walking, and so do I.

"We're here," she says, staring into my eyes. I know she's not going to answer, so I look around us and see nothing. I wonder if the ground is going to open up, or maybe a ladder will lower and I'll be able to walk to heaven.

"No," she says, "I'm more than divine. You and I are the same."

"Huh?" I'm more than confused. "I've noticed that our features are exactly the same. Are you my Enuian *doppelgänger*?"

Adore pets my cheek with the back of her hand. "We are intuitive creatures, you and I. My heart tells me that it is not the time to give you answers. But you will receive them, in due time. Now…" There's a shift in her mood. "You are an Encaser."

"I'm thinking encasing means being able to actually be in someone else."

"Yes, but have you truly been someone else?"

I keep my pondering concealed. I must admit it's mentally exhausting.

"If so, you would taste what the encased tastes. Feel their pains and elations. If they touch something hot, you feel it. If they jump, you rise with them."

"And if they die?" I ask for some strange reason.

"You will not die."

"Oh," I say, not sure whether I'm elated or disappointed. I used to want to escape from my body by any means necessary—even death. Now, here with Adore, that's changed.

"It's time for you to encase me," she says.

I feel her open up to me. I brace myself and take in a deep breath. I've never invaded an individual on purpose. But this time, feeling perfectly safe, I do it.

I become part of Adore. She has a tranquil soul, if it is a soul. Being her is like spending eternity with goodness. I mean, she's so pure that I don't think she's ever felt or thought a bad thing.

Still encased within her, I hear her say, "Come with me."

Before I can ask, "Where to," I feel as if my feet are no longer on the ground. We move with the air, traveling across wide seas of shimmering white, green, and purple rock and mountains made of crystal. They have edifices in this world too. The architecture is Moorish, with its designed arches and columns and straight lines. The cement constructs glow blue, then red, then yellow, then orange. As we fly over them, I wonder what purpose they serve.

In Earth distance, this is probably like traveling from Manhattan to Sydney in less than a minute. We end up in a forest so thick the sun doesn't penetrate the leaves. It's dark, shadowy, and it sounds of hollow nothingness.

"This is the Garden of Naught," she says as she walks its dry grass.

"It's beautiful," I say. Compared to the earth, it is. But something else is going on here. I see Adore's feet tread the ground but not mine. "Wait, am I invisible?"

"You've encased me. Right now, your corporeal self is still at the Field of Dreams, but your inner self is here with me. The reason you're able to do this is because an Encaser's spirit and soul is stronger than the body."

Adore moves deeper into the woods, and I look around in awe. It's so green here that it doesn't even look real. All of a sudden, there's a blast of color. It's so amazing that I stop Adore to look around. Trees hold bushels of leaves that are actually colors, like pink and silver and clear as glass. There's a cool mist in the air and on the ground. The dampness slides through our toes but doesn't stick to our skin. I seek within Adore, and I see that her mouth is turned down and her eyes dull.

"What's wrong?" I ask, shocked by her reaction to all of this beauty.

"There's no life here," she whispers.

I nod. "I know." Even with the brilliant colors and trees, the air is stiff and sound is depleted.

"Enu is without a Life Tree."

"You said something about my blood being from the tree of life?" I shiver at how scary that sounds.

"Look far out," she says.

I look down the path we just left. It was, not long ago, bordered between trees with green leaves. Now there are more colors.

"See, the Tree of Life is what's missing from Enu. But now that we're here, we've brought its life force with us," she says.

I have a couple of questions, but one wins out over the others. "But I'm not really here, right?"

"You've encased me. You are everywhere I go. At least for now."

"What do you mean by 'for now'?"

"When you decide to give yourself to us completely, then you can travel just like me."

"When you say give myself to 'us' completely, do you mean remain here in Enu?" I ask.

"No, you don't have to remain here in Enu to give yourself to us. Although—" She stops herself from elaborating further. "The windows in your quarters are a reflection of your soul."

I think about the scene beyond my windows. The bedroom, bathroom, and the city view are all the things I have affection for.

"The earth holds your heart," she says.

"Isn't this place, Enu, part of the earth? I only went down a few flights of stairs to get here."

She laughs. "Enu is not above or beneath the earth. We have our own galaxies."

"I see," I say as the next question hits me. "You said this place is the Garden of Naught. Why did you bring me here?"

"I'll show you."

Before I know it, we're hovering above the forest. I watch the spot of color slowly fade from the trees.

Adore says, "When we're in the forest, our life force is like the Tree of Life, which is not here."

"I've heard of the Tree of Life, though I'm not a religious person. It's mentioned in the Bible as part of the Garden of Eden. Are you saying this tree really exists? Still?"

"It does exist. There are many of them." Adore sounds quite sure of herself.

"Why hasn't anyone found one then? Humans, I mean the people on Earth, are quite advanced in these things."

"No human eyes will ever see it. No human will ever touch it. They cannot live eternally. The body dies; that is man's lot. The Tree of Life is for those who aren't going to die."

We're back in the garden and standing near the edge of a gaping hole in the ground.

"But you don't have the Tree of Life either," I say.

"No." She sounds sad. "But one day it will grow here, when all the right choices are made."

"So, am I one of those with a choice to make?"

"You are, Cl'auta."

I nod. I understand. Cl'auta means Clarity. Adore's soft approach begins to make sense.

"Free will," I whisper.

"Free will," she concurs.

When my brief trip is over, I go eat a pancake-styled bread topped with the glazed berries and cream. I notice we're still the only ones in the café, but this time Adore joins me in eating.

"Can you tell me anything about yourself?" I ask, chowing down greedily.

Adore seems guarded. "What would you like to know?"

"Do you have parents?"

"Yes."

I pause before taking a bite. "Were you born of a, I don't know"—I stare into my plate because I feel stupid asking this—"a woman and man, male and female?"

"Yes, I was."

I look at her. "Do you know who your parents are?"

"Yes, I do."

I eat some more. I wonder about a lot of things, but the main question I want to ask is on the tip of my tongue. "What about me?"

"You have a mother and father," she confirms.

I look into her face. "I know it's not Freda and Felix. Do you know who?"

"Freda is not your mother," is all she says and stares into my eyes.

"Does that mean Felix *is* my father?"

"Yes," she answers in a whisper, as if she's made a mistake revealing that to me.

I think about our distant relationship, how he's always traveling on business. Not only is he always physically absent, but emotionally too. I would have thought Freda was my real parent, not Felix. "What about my mother? Is she here in Enu?"

Adore shuts her eyes tightly.

I keep pushing. "Is she alive?"

"I apologize, Cl'auta, but I've already said too much."

"I understand," I say with a smile. The last thing I want to do is make Adore uncomfortable. I hold my smile until she looks at me and smiles back. Then I feel cheerfulness fill her again.

After the meal, Adore and I drink cups and cups of Goshem tea. We laugh at the lighter things, such as why I called the Wek a butterfly. I learn that they have no insects or animals in Enu.

"Why?" I ask.

"I don't know," she answers. "That's just how things are."

When I return to my cottage, I sit in a chair and

stare at the cityscape. Why am I so fascinated by skyscrapers? I could never pinpoint the reason. Maybe because, unlike people, each one is determinately opposite the next. This one is constructed in tinted blue mirror glass and shaped like a three-leaf clover, another like a short-legged horseshoe. Then there are gray clay-colored ones, stacked high with pinpoint tops. There are the rose-tinted ones. One always dominates its neighbors in height if not in width. My ability to *encase* has taught me that people aren't as assorted as structures, not as mysterious.

The clouds lording over the city are low and black. Rain pounds the surface. Traffic's at a standstill, and people are power walking to their destinations. I know outside in Enu, the day is more perfect than Earth will ever see.

I walk up to the window and press both hands against the glass. I close my eyes and imagine myself trekking down the sidewalk with no umbrella. I think of Baron. I see his face.

We're sitting by the fire that's lit in this now-nippy living room. *I love the nippiness.* I have a white sweater shawl draped around my shoulders. He's wearing dark gray slacks, and the sleeves of his custom-made shirt are rolled up to his elbows.

We're laughing about my early-childhood television-watching habits. He thinks it's hilarious that I still remember every episode of *Kung-Fu Theater*. I tell him my first sculpture was of Bruce Lee—and I'm not kidding. He laughs harder. I want to kiss him. My body is burning. I want him to consume me, even if that means drinking my blood and taking my life. I want him.

Wham… The window shakes so violently I take one large step back as my eyes open. I'm sure I'm not imagining this, but Baron is pinned against the window. His eyes are blood-red, and the skin beneath them is deep purple. He's so white that it looks as though he's been dipped in flour.

After the shock passes and I'm able to take a step forward, I see he's shivering and his lips are trembling. I think he sees me. I put my hand over his, and his eyes appear to look at my fingers. My palm and fingers are warm. The city is no longer there; it's replaced by a dark, dusty cave. I see the shadow of a human body against the gritty wall behind him. Just as his eyes look into mine, he mouths, "Clarity," and it all disappears.

My heart is pounding, and I'm only seconds away from passing out. Why didn't I encase him?

Maybe I could've. I'm sure that was him in the present, somewhere out there on the verge of death.

"Clarity."

I jump in a panic, and when I turn around, Adore is standing in the doorway.

"I think Baron's in trouble," I mutter past my tight throat.

She stares at me with sad eyes because she already knows my decision.

SIXTEEN

Adore and I are in the bedroom. I'm getting dressed.

You are safe here in Enu, but on the earth, you're not," she says.

I glance at her as I zip up my skirt. Her eyes plead with me to stay, but I can't. If there's a way to help a soul, even an already damned one, I must. The fact that it's Baron's makes it more pertinent that I go and fast.

"Can I help him?" I ask.

She's silent for so long that I try to go into her to see what's turning in her head.

"No!" she shouts.

I feel myself flying across the floor until my back

knocks against the window. For the first time, I'm scared of her.

"There are things I can't tell you. If I do, I could ruin everything." Her voice trembles.

I struggle to my feet, looking at her as if she's some dangerous, beautiful and yet meek thing. "Ruin what?"

Her eyes fill with tears. "I cannot say but one day you will know."

I study her for a while, realizing she still hadn't answered my question. "Still. Can I help him?"

Adore looks away. "Yes."

I nod. That's all I need to know for now.

Adore walks over and takes my hands. I hear a rumble, and though everything around us shakes, my feet stay grounded. The walls of my cottage vanish until we're standing in a vast open field. There are no other cottages or trees, just miles and miles of grass in all four directions.

"What happened?" I ask.

"You created your environment, but now you're leaving it."

"I don't understand."

"Yes, you do."

That is the truth. I loved cottages and silver streams and fluffy green trees under a late-afternoon sun. Enu reminded me of places I used to long to visit from the first time I heard the song "The Candy Man." I let Adore back into my mind to ask my next question. I fear if I speak, my voice will betray me. I want to bawl. I feel like if I leave Enu, then I crush Adore's hopes.

Will I see you again? I ask her. I don't want to *never* see her again. I want to know her forever.

She smiles that electric smile of hers. "We will see each other always, Cl'auta." She squeezes my hands tighter, and her energy flows through my veins.

It's as though the sun is rising inside me. I feel as if I'm the best person I can ever be. I feel as if I can run a hundred miles per hour, leap over the Empire State Building, crush the Great Wall of China with a single blow.

"You are part Enu, and we have made that part stronger inside of you. It will help you on Earth," she says.

I swallow the sadness trapped in my throat. "Okay," I barely say.

"I will hide you where *the evil* can't find you, but it will sense that your Life Blood has returned to the earth. Because of the choices you have made, it will come looking for you."

I nod, scared out of my skin. I remember the alley and the knife to my throat.

"You could have encased the stranger and made him stop," Adore says, studying my fears. "That is your defense and your weapon. However, sometimes when you use your powers, you open yourself up to being discovered by *the evil*. Keep your powers closed until you need them, and wherever you are when you use them, never stay at that place unless it is protected."

"How will I know if it's protected?"

"I do not know," she says sadly. "I have never felt that universe."

"Do you mean Earth?"

"Yes. I have never been there."

Of course she hasn't. I have questions to ask her, but there's no time. I must get to Baron. "Don't worry about me, Adore. I'll be fine." I squeeze her hands to comfort her.

She smiles. "Are you ready, Clarity?"

I nod.

"Be well my... Cl'auta."

I grimace. I feel as if she was going to say more but chose not to. Suddenly I'm weightless. Bright light ignites in my head and...

CHAPTER
SEVENTEEN

S uddenly, I'm in the middle of a desert. I tilt my head back and see that the sun is directly overhead; it's noon. Though it's hot now, in about two hours, it'll be blistering hot. I soon realize that I'm clutching my purse and my bag. I take out my wallet and count my cash. I have two hundred and thirty dollars, plus all of my credit cards and my driver's license.

I spot a road about fifty yards south, so I trot over to it, kicking up sand along the way. I wonder if I'm still in the United States. I walk up the dusty asphalt road ten minutes later, and there's not a single truck, car, or motorcycle in sight. My toes are sweating in my black pumps, and my throat is dry. I almost blame Adore for dumping me here. If the "evil" doesn't kill me, the heat will.

It soon dawns on me that my hair is down. In Enu, I hardly noticed, but here, I feel as if I'm wearing a fur coat. I want to call on my abilities. With all that I discovered about myself, I'm sure I can get out of this pickle. I'd be a fool if I didn't try. So I close my eyes and feel for any signs of human life.

This must be an off-road away from the main highway because bodies swoop past me at speeds that only a car can go. I encase one of those bodies and look at the person in the rearview mirror. He's a middle-aged man with black hair in a sporty black car. The cool air pushing through his vents glazes over me. I see two suitcases in the backseat, a Porkies Burger cup in the cup-holder, and a cheese-burger on his lap. The scent of the meat makes my stomach turn.

Drink.

He picks up the cold cup and sucks on the straw. I feel the cool lemon-lime drink slide down my throat. The carbonation is strong, but it soothes the dryness. Together we drink it all. I lead him to me, standing here on the deserted road.

I ask him why it's so hot in November.

"It's July," he says, staring out over the road. He appears to be entranced.

I've taken complete control of him, and I do feel bad about that. All my life, I've run away from doing just this, but now that has changed. My survival depends on doing what I hate the most. How can it be nine months later? Could time in Enu pass slower than time on Earth?

Before long, we're at the spot where I'm standing along the side of the road. I have him open the door. My switch has to be swift. I fear that if I leave him, he'll return to himself and panic. I decide to try something that makes sense to me— maybe it'll work.

"You're picking up the lady in the skirt and giving her a ride to safety, okay?" I say.

"Okay," he repeats.

I make it fast. I return all of me to myself and slide into the car. In that moment, the guy has the most confused look I've ever seen. When I encase him again, his thoughts are muddled, caught between wondering who I am and where he is. But he isn't afraid, and for that, I'm relieved.

There's a navigation system on the control panel, and I know that every moment I'm inside him is dangerous. I have it locate the nearest airport, which happens to be in San Angelo, Texas, and only twenty miles away.

Where are you going? I ask him.

"Phoenix."

Do you have a cell phone?

He retrieves it from a holder above the top of the windshield. "It's here." He holds it up.

Can you make a call and drive at the same time?

"Yes."

Call 2-1-2-7-7-9-1-6-8-5.

He makes the call.

After two buzzes, I hear Molly, my father's assistant, say, "Felix Parker's office." She doesn't say, "How may I help you?" of course. Molly never says that.

"Molly," I say, though not in a voice she would recognize.

"Excuse me, but to whom am I speaking?"

My mind works fast; I don't want to tell my second lie ever. "Cl'auta," I have him say. I don't know why, but I can still speak Enu.

Molly is silent for so long that I wonder if she understood what I said. "Molly?"

"Sorry, sir, he's not in, but I'll let him know you called."

Before I can respond, she ends the call. When

we arrive at San Angelo, I thank the man—whose name is Clarence—and remind him that he's on his way to Phoenix. Once I let him go, I rush into the terminal. I've noticed there's a short period of confusion that occurs after I've encased someone, which gives me time to escape. When I turn back, he's massaging his neck and looks around one more time before driving off.

I take a flight to Dallas/Fort Worth and from there to San Francisco, where Felix has a condo. I would love to go back to New York and resume my life, but I know that's no longer an option.

My eyes are heavy, and all I want to do is sleep for a while. This extreme exhaustion hits me out of nowhere and hard, but as we take to the sky, I'm too afraid to close my eyes. I wonder if *the evil* is close to finding me. I encased Clarence for quite some time, and I'm kicking myself for making that huge mistake. Maybe there was another way out of the arid desert. If the airport was only twenty minutes away by car, I probably could've walked there.

I look down at my high designer skirt and black shoes. I'm spoiled. Maybe too spoiled to save Baron's life. Life had become tough, and already I'm clinging to my mommy, who isn't my mom, and daddy. All Felix has to do is check my credit card purchases to see that I'm in San Francisco. What will he do when he finds me? I'm quite sure he won't say, "Let's save the vampire who needs your blood to be free from his thirst." I need to go where he won't find me.

When I get to Dallas/Fort Worth, I use all six credit cards at the ATMs in the airport to get six thousand dollars. The only clothing store I see for women is Brooks Brothers, so I stop there to buy a navy blue-and-white-striped cotton jersey dress and a pair of flat sandals.

Even with the lightweight clothing, I feel as if I'm stepping into a heated skillet when I walk out into Dallas, Texas. The extreme light instantly burns my eyes. I hate the dry heat and the stark light. I'll take the smothering, damp heat the East Coast offers any day. I know I can't stay long. Once Felix finds out I haven't arrived in San Francisco, Dallas will be the next logical place to search. I decide not to take the Trinity Railroad Express from the airport to the main Amtrak station. Instead, I take a cab.

It's time to find Baron, and my instincts are telling me to go to a place where no one thinks I'll ever go. In a cab ride to the train station, I think of where those places might be. I'd never go to Alaska,

Montana, the Dakotas, or anywhere in the Midwest. I would go to Washington, DC, New York, Connecticut, Massachusetts, or anywhere on the east and southeast coast.

"Not staying long?" the cab driver asks, interrupting my thoughts.

I glance at him through the rearview mirror. He's waiting for my response.

"No," I say.

"That's too bad. We can always use another pretty lady in Dallas." His chuckle sounds like a frog croaking.

"Oh." I turn to look out the window, trying to avoid having a discussion.

He's still sizing me up through the rearview mirror. "Where are you from?"

"California." That's true, even though I haven't been there since graduating from high school.

"Cl'auta," he says.

Every muscle in my body tenses. "What did you say?" My pulse races.

EIGHTEEN

"Gek'tu, namek, benuk, du'hi, du'jek, du'zek, rak'u Irving."

I spring forward and grab the driver's seat. "Felix?" I can no longer feel my father near, so I push back into my seat and wait for the cab driver to gather his bearings. When he finally does, I say, "I need you to go to 4590 Irving Highway."

The rest of the ride is quiet. I see the cab driver is a bit frightened by what happened to him. The person who's been encased actually loses that time. As soon as he came to, he looked out of all his windows and then at me. I avoided eye contact, but I could tell he was still leery of me.

The place Felix leads me to is a storage center.

That warmth, the one that I felt in Enu, washes over me as soon as I step out of the cab. This must be what protection feels like. I'm not happy that I ended up doing what my "daddy" said to do. I'm sure he's not happy with me right now. Felix has never been one for chastising or lectures. When I look back on my days with him, I realize that for the most part, I've always bent easily to his will—and I wonder if I ever truly had the option of choosing.

I walk into the office. A pretty, petite brown girl with a cropped haircut is behind the counter. She looks at me with the initial jolt most have at first sight.

"Hi," she says, being sure to give me a Texas-style greeting. "How can I help you?"

I wonder if I just say it. I check over both shoulders. "Benuk gek."

Without another word, she walks over to a file cabinet and digs out a plastic file folder that zips. Two keys are attached to a small black control box inside it.

"A45 is already open." She fishes out the keys and gives them to me. "Here you go."

I take it. "Is that it?"

"Yes, ma'am. Thank you," she says and gives me the standard smile.

When I get to the shed and lift the aluminum door, I see a silver BMW with black-tinted windows inside. I use the key to open the door, and the alarm goes off. It sounds like a high-pitched foghorn. I fumble with the keys and hit buttons until it stops. When I get into the car, I take the little black box off the key ring and shut it in the glove compartment. No need to fuss with the alarm any longer.

With the protection over this facility, I know the time has come for me to do the inevitable. I feel a pinch of fear, but there's no putting it off. Every second I lose can be fatal for Baron.

I close my eyes and recall Baron's touch—the way his hand ran across the small of my back as we stood in the gallery six years ago, examining the ultra-phallic piece of clay stuck on a log. I like the fact that he was actually giving the piece the old postgraduate try. Even though I couldn't penetrate his thoughts and emotions, it was apparent he was deliberating and trying to figure it out.

"This guy is mocking us," Baron said, offering his final assessment.

I think that's the moment I wanted to be with him in whatever capacity he'd have me. Then later on the bridge, his lips felt like warm butter dripping down my neck. Even now my entire body ignites from just thinking about it.

It's subtle, but I'm sure I've found him because I'm in a cave. It's so dark in here. I imagine it's cold, but all I feel is warmth. My muscles are energized and so strong, I feel as though if I push the dusty wall, it'll come tumbling down. The only problem is I don't see my hands or feet. Those limbs are not with me—none of my limbs are with me—yet I'm here and not encased inside him.

I hear water moving very slowly. It's a pool of water, actually. There's definitely a scent of condensation. More than that, I feel him near.

Baron, I call.

Faintly, I hear him gasp my name. I call again.

This time he says, *Clarity*.

He's near. I move through a narrow gap. If I were physically present, I'd have to shuffle in sideways. Once I get through the gap, I see him pressed against the wall and slumped over.

I can't believe my eyes. What look like daggers are stuck in each of his thighs and in the right side of his chest. His skin is the color of chalk, lips so dry they're cracked, and he has two black eyes. He looks so weak, but he finds the strength to lift his face.

"Clarity," he mutters.

Do you see me? I ask.

"How did you get here?"

I wanted to come to you, so I thought about you. Can you see me?

He's so out of it, I wonder if he knows what's going on.

"I need your warmth. Come and touch me if you're here."

I hesitate.

"Hurry before…"

I rush over before the "before" happens. I can't see myself, but I know I'm kneeling, and my right hand caresses his face. I think it's God whom I'm thanking for finding him alive. He takes me by my wrist, or where my wrist would be.

Whatever this energy is hits me hard. I wonder if I should pull away, but I see the color returning to his skin. Deep grunts come from his throat as he grinds his teeth. He says something to me when he pulls the first dagger out of his chest and casts it aside. It sounds like "coming." Then he pulls the daggers out of his thighs.

The dark shadow from when I saw Baron close to death in Enu has returned. I look over my shoulder and see a male and female coming at

Baron with more daggers. Baron shoots to his feet. He seems to stand ten feet tall, ready for whatever they throw at him. The guy rushes him with the dagger, and one moment Baron's there, and then he's not. His opponent stops cold. He bears down over me, but I'm sure he can't see me.

His brows knit together, and he sniffs. "She's here!"

Baron descends on him with one of the daggers from his thighs. In one clean swipe, I become privy to the most horrific sight I've ever seen. I can't look away from the guy's head detached from his body. Now Baron's facing down the girl. She's also sniffing the air, keeping her distance from him.

"Ze Feldis," she says with an Eastern European accent, "we could have her together. We will never thirst again."

I'm frozen where I sit. I wonder what he's thinking.

"Or we can use her as leverage and neither of us drink her," she says, sniffing and looking in my direction.

I push myself deeper into the wall.

"You're not hers, Ze Feldis. Let's kill her together. You and me."

"It's *you* I'm going to kill, Zina Osgard," Baron says.

"Not before I kill her," Zina growls.

Before I know it, she's gone—so fast it seems as if she disappeared into thin air. I can tell he wants to give chase, but he doesn't.

Clarity, are you really here? he asks.

No, I'm not, I respond.

But how?

I don't know.

Then he flicks his face toward the circular opening. He appears on edge, alarmed. *Let's meet in Cambridge.* He's gone.

When I open my eyes, I'm back in the car, facing a row of flat five-by-ten storage spaces with aluminum doors. The sunlight trapped in the middle of the quad stuns me.

I cut on the engine, press my foot on the accelerator, and shoot out of the tiny garage too fast. I slam on the brakes before I can crash into someone's storage space. I haven't driven in ten years. I take a deep breath, grip the steering wheel, and ease my foot onto the gas pedal. I'm off.

CHAPTER
NINETEEN

B y the time I reach Memphis, it's seven o'clock at night and I can hardly keep my eyes open. I notice the navigational system on the dashboard, and I fumble my way through using it to find the Madison Hotel. When I get to the Madison and step into the lobby, I feel a sense of relief. At the same time, I'm nervous. They'll need my credit card and ID, and I can't give them. I do have my corporate card, and I remember a conversation I had with Michael a few years ago about our numbers being the same up to the last four digits. The good thing is I remember the last four digits of his card.

"Welcome to the Madison Hotel," the clerk says as I walk up to the desk.

I encase her immediately. We make my reservation under Michael Colton and use his credit card number. We skip my identification. Before we're finished, another customer steps up behind me.

I look at myself standing still, eyes glazed over. This is the first time I've seen myself up close in this state; I must admit it's sort of odd. I'm vulnerable and at the mercy of whomever or whatever. I hurry things up when another front desk clerk enters and addresses the guy behind me. They both steal looks at the real me.

"Everything okay, Lisa?" the other girl asks.

"Yes," I say through her. When I hand myself the key cards and invoice, Lisa says, "Thank you and enjoy your stay."

I tell myself to take them, and miraculously, I do. I tell myself to head up the stairs, and I turn and do that as well.

As my body walks away, the other girl looks at Lisa and whispers, "Pretty, but weird."

"Yeah, she's tired. Been on the road all day," I make Lisa say.

"Still…" the other girl says.

"Hey, I'll be right back," I say. Lisa and I walk to the back room where there are desks and a bulky copier. I leave her at the very back of the room by a coffeemaker and a basket of hard muffins. When I rejoin myself, I'm standing at the top of the stairs. The mission wasn't perfect but successful. I'm quite proud of myself.

I waste no time getting to my suite, peeling off my clothes, and running a hot bath. I turn on the TV while I wait for the bathtub to fill. Flipping through the channels, I stop on a news report. Thick fog has fallen over the streets of San Francisco. It's caused fourteen major traffic accidents, and the Golden Gate Bridge and the Oakland Bay Bridge have been closed. Already lunatic preachers are predicting judgment over the city.

I think my heart has stopped because I know what's really going on. I can sense them there in the fog, searching. I flick the TV off, get into the tub, bathe as fast as I can, and get into the bed. Before I know it, I'm out—I think.

I'm lying in bed on my back, arms along my sides. My eyes are open, and I'm staring at the top of a cave. Somewhere in the distance, I hear water pouring into a deep pool. A woman is singing a poem of some sort.

Don't try to run from me.
I'll feed your heart to the sea.
You drink her blood to the end.

Then be human again!

Her laugh sounds like a cackle, and she's getting close. I'm cold down to my icy feet. A presence stands at the left side of my bed, lording over me. I can't move. I can't scream. I can't look. When I gasp for air, I believe she's choking me. Cold lips press against my neck and something sharp punctures my skin. I try to cry out. I try to use my ability to stop her, but my entire body is like a Popsicle. I call out for Baron, struggling against the stagnant force. That's when my eyes pop open, and I sit up. The sun has lightened the room, and I'm alone. I sigh, thankful it was only a nightmare.

It's ten o'clock in the morning. My head is cloudy, and the tension in my neck is tight. That nightmare was so vivid. I wonder if that's my fate. Will this Zina have my head?

I click on the television to *Headline News* to see if any more strange fog is being reported. I see it's all clear here in Memphis. I want to open the curtains and look out over the harbor, but I'm too afraid. I'm afraid of everything now, but I know once I'm with Baron again, a lot of the fear will subside.

I'm brushing my teeth when I hear there's now thick fog in Phoenix, New York, and Cambridge. It cleared out of San Francisco at exactly 8:59 p.m.

PDT. Some are wondering if it's some sort of terrorist attack and debating whether or not people should be tested. I wonder if they'd have me committed if I tried to explain the phenomenon.

I get dressed quickly and head out of the room. Downstairs, there are too many people at the front desk for me to pay cash. Lang, Bender & Jenison will get the bill. I'm sure they'll count it as an accounting error. Incorrect billing happens so often there because some *genius* asked the bank to make the credit card numbers tight for accounting purposes.

CHAPTER

TWENTY

The drive up I-40 during the late afternoon proves to be grueling stop-and-go traffic. I'm determined to drive on without stopping other than to gas up and eat. For the most part, I can do both at one stop, surviving off of water, water, and more water. I find that off-highway food makes my stomach turn.

When darkness falls again, I wonder if Baron has made it to Cambridge yet. Then I wonder how. Someone who moves as fast as he does wouldn't need to drive. He's an actual vampire. I really haven't dealt with that reality yet. My first encounter with vampires was Halloween in third grade.

Chester Lowenthau donned a black cape and

fake fangs with red gel on them and chased the girls around the classroom, declaring in a fake accent, "I vant to drink your blood!" He never chased me, of course, because he was afraid of me. All the kids in my class were. Kids have stellar intuition. They knew one of their peers was a different being. They couldn't quite put a finger on what I was, but they knew I was something different. Heck, I knew I was something peculiar, and it scared me too!

The early sun is rising as I take Exit 18 off the I-90E. Something on the car keeps me from having to stop to pay tolls; I roll right on through. I'm only fifty miles away from Cambridge, and I'm pressing my teeth together to stop them from chattering. The frightening fog lingers ahead.

I wonder where Felix is. Where's Viesel Egos? And isn't Freda my *guardian*? Where are my guardians? I thought I wanted to do this alone, but after that dream, I've wholeheartedly reclaimed my dependent mindset.

The good thing is I'm back to the part of the country I love the most. I try to roll down the windows to smell the oak, maple, and apple trees, but the glass won't budge. I guess it's because of the protection.

I arrive an hour later. Driving through

Cambridge is a chore because I can barely see one foot ahead of me. The sidewalks are practically bare. It looks as though most people have decided to stay inside today, afraid of the vapor. As I stop at a light on Broadway—and maybe my eyes are deceiving me—I see black shadows sweep across the sidewalks and up and down the sides of buildings. They seem to be searching, and because of the jolts of terror I feel, I know they are adversarial.

When I see my old building up ahead, I notice there are no black shadows crawling around it. *That's a relief.* I pull up to the gate to the subterranean parking, trying to figure out how I could open it. Lo and behold, it lifts automatically. I drive through and park in the space dedicated to our condo.

I sit at the steering wheel contemplating my next move. Should I or shouldn't I take the protection with me? I don't know if it worked in Memphis. I remember when I walked the hallways at the Manhattan apartment during the fog and how my neighbors stood outside their doors to peer at me as if we were stuck in an episode of the *Twilight Zone.* I close my eyes and wrap myself in some of the car's protection. I notice that it's weaker than it was in Memphis. I wonder if the fog tried to eat at it or if my taking from it depletes it. Instead, to be safe, I take from a stronger source— the building.

The power is overwhelming and pins me to the black leather seat. When I think I've gotten enough, I let go and rush out of the car. I feel as though I can run a hundred miles at a hundred miles per hour. My feet barely touch the ground, like being in Adore's body. I race up twenty-six flights of stairs instead of taking the elevator, and when I get to the top, I'm not even close to being out of breath.

As I step into the hallway, my heart stops. I'm faced with the same scene as in New York, but the neighbors are standing in their doorways looking toward our door. I take a deep breath to gather strength. I must face the eeriness alone. All I hear are my flat shoes pressing cautiously across the black marble floor. As I pass, they look on as if they can't see me. Even when I turn the knob, finding the door already unlocked, they stare in my direction, but past me.

My heart goes into overdrive after I close and lock the door behind me. He's facing me. My knees are weak, and though I feel as though I'm floating, I also feel as though I'm falling. Before I can form one word, he's in front of me, pulling me into him.

His hands caress the small of my back, and I merge into the warmth again. My head is spinning.

I can finally breathe. "You're here."

That's when Baron presses his lips against mine. The merging is soft and careful. I wonder if he can feel my pulse racing and heart knocking. His chest is solid, his arms strong. Finally, I feel safe, even if in our alien circle of life, he is predator and I'm prey. I want more of him than this. He lets down my hair, gathers a handful, and lifts me off the ground with his other hand. He restrains a growl. I know he's trying not to scare me, but I could never be afraid of him. Whatever he wants from me, I'll freely give.

Not even in the span of one second, he carries me to my old bedroom, and I'm falling on top of the bed. We haven't stopped kissing yet. His face is intense, eyes full of desire. I wonder if he's all there until he smirks at me. *Gosh, I miss that smirk.* I smirk back, and before I know it, he's off of me and I'm lying on top of my old bed alone.

I'm woozy when I walk back into the living room. The place has been redecorated. Baron sits on a burnt orange microfiber sofa. He's leaning forward with his face buried in his hands. I sit beside him. He looks so fragile.

"Baron," I ask, "are you okay?"

"I can't stay here long."

"Well, okay. But—"

"You know more about what I am, don't you?"

"Yes, I know you're a…" I look down at my feet. My shoes are still on. I kick them off. "A vampire."

He stares deep in my eyes. "You would've let me drink you if I had asked. Wouldn't you?"

I hang my head to say, "Yes, I think so."

He caresses my thigh. "You would've. I want you so badly; I don't think I could've stopped myself from taking you."

"You mean you want my blood so bad?"

"Yes, I want your blood. You've felt my thirst, haven't you?"

Indeed, I remember how my throat felt as if it was cracking into a million pieces.

"Can you imagine living with that for an eternity?"

"Yes, I can," I whisper.

He pauses; I can tell he's taken aback by my reply.

Baron cups my chin gently. "But when I touch you, it soothes me." His brows crimp, and he looks off into the foggy night. "I don't know why that is.

Do you?" He looks at me again. His eyes are hypnotizing.

I can't speak, so I shake my head.

"I'm making you uncomfortable? I'm sorry," he says.

"No, you can never make me feel like that," I assure him.

We're silent. I look out the window with him. Just that fast, all of the fog has lifted, giving way to the full night.

"I was a prince. Next to rule the house of Ze Feldis, but you would've thought I was already king. That's how I behaved at least. I was a jackass."

"No," I say. "You can never be that."

"I was, Clarity, and I will never let you meet that guy." A faraway look clouds his eyes. "On the day before I became *this*, a vampire, my brothers and I invaded a village in the Highlands and killed three men because Luco, one of my brothers, claimed he saw one of them pissing on the walls of my inherited kingdom. 'You can't have him doing that,'" Baron says with a sneer, mimicking his brother. "Can you believe I took a man's life for pissing on a wall a million men had pissed on before him?"

I don't know what to say. I've run across the heart of a man or woman who would do something like that. Sometimes vile acts come from a very shallow place.

"He begged me not to do it. He said he had children and a wife."

I can see he's far away again.

"I went to the brothel to drink and screw the entire despicable ordeal away." He stops to remember it. "I guess what goes around comes around. Do you know about the mant-hanans?"

"No," I say, jolted by the change of subject.

"I once heard that your kind call them *the evil*."

"You said my kind? Did you always know? About me?"

"I don't know what you are exactly. But you have the Blood of Life."

I walk over to stand face to face with him, and his strong hands pull me into him again. My touch soothes Baron Ze Feldis. The warmth we share is not stirred up by emotions; it's a true physical reaction.

"Have you ever come across other people like me?" I ask.

He presses his cheek against mine. "Once."

I want to ask him what happened, but a dreadful feeling stops me.

"I want you to know that you shouldn't trust me

as much as you do, Clarity. I want your blood, but I want *you* more. If we go in there"—he points toward the bedroom with his chin—"and I fully give in to my need for you…" He holds me tighter. "You have to keep your head. You can keep me from killing you, but you have to keep your head."

"I'll try. But it may be impossible." It *truly* may be.

We stand like this for a while. Baron Ze Feldis, once known to me as Baron Ford, doesn't have a heartbeat. There's no sign that this tower of man is alive.

"I have to stop Zina before she sends colonies of vampires after you," he says.

"That sounds serious." My arms still hold on tight to him.

"We all want to be free of this eternal thirst."

"I'm only one person. How can a colony of vampires drink one person?"

He sniffs with a chuckle. "They'll slay each other until the last monster is standing."

"Interesting," is all I say.

He looks at me with that smirk again. "What are you thinking?" Baron gazes into my eyes.

I press my cheek onto his hollow chest to avoid looking into his. "Well, at first I thought maybe we should use me as bait to let them destroy themselves by trying to get to me. But then I remembered they were all once human. And don't all human beings deserve redemption?"

"Didn't you hear my story?" He almost sounds a bit angry. "I killed an innocent man! I was a monster even as a human. Every vampire I've ever met was a subpar human being as well."

"I don't think you're the judge of that." There's a bite in my tone.

"You're right. Circumstance is."

I shake my head. "What do you think the brothel was about?"

He appears to have an inner struggle. "There's no hope for me," he whispers at last.

This time, I initiate the kiss. It's the tenderest merging of two mouths, and I'm floating under his spell. I pull back. "What next?"

"I need to know what's going on. They're looking for you, but you're safe as long as you stay here."

"No. I'm not staying here while you're out there."

"This is not an arguable point."

"I know." I let go of him. "And really, there are holes in your plan."

"What holes in my plan?"

I smile a bit. I didn't know vampires could feel insulted. "Well, let's see. Two vampires had you in a cave, drained of strength and on the verge of death."

"I wasn't going to die; I'm already dead."

"Don't they know we're…"—I stop to the think of a word—"tuned in to each other already?"

I hope he's as tuned in to me as I am to him. If he leaves, within five minutes, my heart will crave his company, my body his touch. I cannot be without Baron Ze Feldis.

He sits on the sofa again. "Zina definitely knows you and I are together."

I mask my sigh of relief before sitting beside him. He does consider us "tuned in" to each other. That's good.

"I can go with you. I've learned how to bring the protection with me. See?" I stand and race from one side of the room to the other faster than humanly possible. Before I know it, he's facing me.

"Clarity, what in this world are you?"

"Well…I don't know." That's the sad truth. I have no idea what I am, but I am something. He touches my shoulder with those powerful hands of his, and I feel safe enough to admit, "Maybe I'm a little Enuian, I think."

"Enuian?" He says that as though the word is completely foreign to him.

"Well, it's a place. It's where I was when you first came to me."

"I came to you?"

"I was there when I saw you in the cave."

I see him working to remember.

"It's all foggy," he admits.

"Well, you were in bad shape."

"And you left that place to come to me?" His entire face frowns.

I don't know if he thinks that's a good thing or a bad thing. I nod. I don't think I could stand it if he'd rather I stayed there.

Baron lifts my chin with his index finger, lowers his mouth to mine, and our lips press together. They feel warm and soft, and we're sharing a perfect kiss. His hands are at the small of my back again, pulling me into him. He whisks me off the sofa, and we move at what seems like the speed of light toward the bedroom.

I'm lying on top of the bed, and he slips my dress off over my head. He pulls back to take in the sight of me in my black panties and bra. I've never felt so beautiful in my life—never wanted to feel this beautiful. When he closes his eyes and clenches his jaw, I can see that he's aroused.

"You are…" he says and then forces his eyes off me. "I don't know if I can do this."

"You don't have to," I barely say. I don't even convince myself with that claim. He definitely has to. There's no going back. Our desire is too strong. Every sensitive part of me is pulsating.

He slides a hand up my inner thigh, causing me to catch my breath. His eyes are focused on his hand. He's breathing heavily by the time his fingers reach the point where all my sensations are, and I exhale deeply. He just presses his finger on a spot, presses and circles it. I suck air. The sensations build until I feel the explosion. I cry out.

How could he do that?

When I open my eyes, he's staring at my face. Without hesitation, he does it again.

"Oh my God." I whimper. I soon feel the explosion and whimper. What a sensation. I have never…

"What are you doing?" I ask while panting.

"Your face is sexy," he whispers thickly.

I manage to prop myself up on my elbows. "I guess you learn a few tricks by being around so long." I wear a coy grin.

He sniffs and smirks. "Like you said, we're tuned in to each other." Then he stands at the foot of my bed. "It's going to take some time before I'm able to have you completely. I still want you too much, and I might—"

"I know," I say and move toward him.

"No." He holds up a hand to stop me. "Do you have something to wear here?"

Still breathing heavily, I force myself to look toward the closet. Both it and the drawers are loaded with the stuff Freda bought me, clothes I've never worn. "Yes, but it's all high designer." I scoot off the bed and notice he's not looking at my face but my body. I open the bottom drawer of the solid oak dresser and pull out a pair of overwashed jeans and a white tank top. "I have my sculpting clothes here."

"Good." He tears his eyes away from me. "Put them on."

Before I know it, he's out of the room. His disappearing acts are something I'll probably never get used to.

He's still avoiding full-on eye contact with me when I walk back into the living room. I know my nipples are standing on edge, so I cross my arms to hide them.

"Okay, what's next?" I ask.

He whips across the floor, stuffs a piece of paper in my hand, and kisses me with controlled restraint. I close my eyes and dream of how he touched me just minutes ago.

"I'll meet you here," he whispers in my ear.

"But aren't we going to stay together?" Like an idiot, I ask this with my eyes closed. When I open them, he's gone.

TWENTY-ONE

N ow alone, I unfold the paper Baron put in my hand. An address in Veil Green, Massachusetts, is written on it. Thinking two steps ahead, I stuff another pair of jeans and fresh underwear into my bag. Something tells me I'll be gone for a while.

When I walk out of the condo, I see that the neighbors have gone inside. They're probably watching their televisions, whipping up tonight's dinner, clicking away on their computers, or actually having conversations. Part of me wishes Baron and I could be that normal, but the other part knows that's not in the least bit viable. He's a vampire from another period in time. He can move like the wind, and he fights like a comic book superhero.

The elevator ride to the parking garage goes smoothly. Down here, all of my senses are heightened. I drive out of the parking structure. Though the fog has lifted, it's still an uneasy night. The sky is hazy, there's no moon in sight, and it's sort of chilly for a July night in Cambridge. I make all the turns the GPS advises me to take until I'm out of the city and on the highway heading east.

I've never heard of Veil Green, but apparently the navigational system has. Driving in the dark, I try to put it all in perspective. As it stands, the details are scattered and not much really makes sense. The dominant points are Baron's a vampire, Freda's not my mother, and Felix is my father. This leads to a few other questions, such as how did I come to be and who's my mother. I think I was once an infant, even though I've never seen one baby picture of myself. I always thought it was because Freda and Felix weren't sentimental.

Then I remember how Aries was around more than my parents were. She clearly cared for me, but she never said much to me other than, "Ready?" Or, "Are you hungry?" Or, "What time should I pick you up?" That time I cut my hair, her face didn't even drop. She just smiled at me and went back to playing in the water with her boyfriend. She had to have known that it would grow back. What's up with the hair anyway? Adore has the same type of hair.

On the secondary list of facts—these creatures, Selells or vampires, want to drink my blood, possibly to be restored. Baron cannot make love to me because he also desires to drain me. Now that my existence is known to the "vampire community," they're going to forever hunt me because I'm like an icy martini on a scorching hot day. Finally, Baron needs to stop Zina or thousands of other vampires, whichever poses the direct threat.

Then there are the mysteries. Why does Baron's ice-cold skin warm up every time he touches me? Why does the protection guard me from *the evil* and every vampire except Baron? Maybe because I invite him to me, that neutralizes the defenses.

Also, where in the world is Felix, my father? He guides me to the car, and then I never hear from him? I'm not surprised, but I am disappointed. How stupid of me to think with all that I know now, our relationship would change.

My eyes are watery, but something inside me refuses to let me cry. That would make it harder to see the road. It's extra dark because of the trees lording over it, and the pitch-black woods are scary. Thoughts of Felix will have to require my tears another time, under less frightening circumstances. I switch on the high beams, and that helps a little, but only a little.

I'm not sure, but up ahead, the road looks as though it's a dead end. I slow down, creeping forward. When I get closer, I see the tree line ahead is just as dense as the ones beside the road. It *is* a dead end.

"What the," I whisper.

I have no idea what to do next other than make a U-turn and zoom back to civilization. Before I can pull the gear into reverse, a white figure steps from between the tree trunks in front of the car. My heart stops, and I feel myself actually jump. It only takes a second to realize it's Baron. I push the door open and run to his arms.

He squeezes me tightly but releases me quicker than usual. "We can't linger."

I bob my head in agreement. There's something menacing in the air. It's unseen at the moment, but it or they are all around us. "Okay, so do you want to get in the car?"

He grins. "As you can see, there isn't a road ahead of us."

My face drops. "Oh."

"Are you ready?"

"Ready for what?"

"To go."

"But what about the car?"

"We don't need the car."

"Oh." I know I'm holding us up. I believe he wants me to march into those dark, scary woods. "Where's Veil Green? I don't think we're there yet."

"I'm going to take you the rest of the way." He grins at me. "Are you afraid?"

"No." That was a quick answer and a lie told too easily. I am scared. I pretend to be brave and reach into the car to grab my bag. After making sure the doors are locked, I say, "All right, let's get it over with."

He studies me with a grin and then looks down at my bag before taking my free hand. "I'm not going to let anything happen to you."

"I know," I say with a sigh.

Him keeping me safe is not the problem—him *having* to keep me safe is the problem. Before I know it, we are gliding along at a remarkable speed. I had no idea I could travel like this on Earth. I can't see anything in the pitch-black woods, but I smell the dampening soil. Every now and then, I feel the light slap of leaves against my face. At first, nothing can be heard except the sound of air passing. Then a screeching scream echoes throughout the forest.

Baron stops cold and pulls me into him. This is a new kind of hug, a protective one. "They're here."

His lips touch my ear. He doesn't breathe. I know that for sure now.

"We need your covering."

"You mean the protection?" I whisper back.

"Yes. Hurry, they're getting closer." He pulls me tighter, and in a second, we're off the ground and surrounded by branches, hiding in the bulk of the foliage.

I try what has worked so far. I find the energy from the car and pull on it.

When warmth surrounds us, I say, "I did it."

We drop out of the trees and onto the thistly ground. There's more yelling and screams of pain. Actual bodies jet past us. I want to ask Baron what's happening, but then I see Viesel Egos. His blue eyes are glowing, and he's wielding that sword that looks to be on fire. He twists it and slices upward. There's another cry. Then in the next move, that blade is against Baron's neck.

"Get her out of the forest," Viesel Egos growls. He looks at me. I can tell he's not happy. "Out of the forest!"

He continues the fight. Baron cradles me, and I don't even think I blink before we're moving through the branches. We end up on the doorstep of a Tudor-styled gray brick house in the middle of nowhere.

TWENTY-TWO

Baron puts me down and glares toward the forest with a snarl. "That's the second time he's put a blade to my throat."

The lack of love between Baron and Viesel Egos is pretty apparent.

"I'm sorry about that," I say as I look out over the lay of the land. The house is set in the middle of a clearing. The surrounding woods are so far away that the trees look like short hedges in the distance.

"Don't apologize for what he does."

The door opens just in time to eliminate the awkward moment.

"You made it," the man, whom I recognize as Dr. Herbert Dove, says.

Baron's teeth are still clenched. "Yes."

Dr. Dove examines me. "You must be Clarity."

He has a unique appearance. I didn't get a good look at him six years ago because I was too focused on the beautiful guy to my right. Dr. Dove has a full head of white hair, but his face looks, at most, thirty years old. He's very pale but with a hint of a tan undertone, giving him an almost royal appearance. His eyebrows are jet black, and so are his eyes. And his physique is strong and vital.

"I am," I say after a long pause.

"Welcome to our home." He steps back to allow me entrance and closes the door behind us.

My eyes can't stop roaming the room. Tall bookcases filled with books cover all four walls. It looks as if this man does nothing but read all day and night. On one side of the room is a massive desk with a large book opened on top of it and a reading light turned on. A large comfy sofa with a chaise lounge connected to it sits in front of an unlit fireplace. Grandfather clocks line one side of the room, and each clock displays a different world time.

"It's a little jarring at first sight, isn't it?" Dr. Dove asks. He has a faint accent, which I'm unable to place.

"It is," I answer with a smile.

"What is a man without his mountain?" He winks and then turns to Baron. "She is all that you reported."

"Is she here?" a lady calls from somewhere upstairs.

I think she's in my head because her energy consumes me, but then her voice fills up the living room. This woman, whoever she is, has a strong presence. My soul, spirit, or whatever is inside me flows to her; we're bonding somehow.

"She's here," Dr. Dove calls, wearing a huge grin.

She appears at the top of the staircase and looks down upon me. Instinctively, I let go of Baron's hand and step toward her.

Oh, Cl'auta, the woman says.

Oh, Falu. How do I know her name is Fawn?

Fawn is a breathtaking creature. Her hair is the same length and texture as mine, but it's the color of orange spice. Her skin is as delicate and white as porcelain, and her eyes are emerald. I hear her assessing my beauty in the same way. I wonder how we can look so different from each other but be carbon copies of each other at the same time. It looks as if we're even the same height, weight, and age. It's amazing.

Are you hungry, Cl'auta? We have a lot to discuss.

I glance at Baron, who's watching us curiously.

"She'll be in your arms soon, Ze Feldis. I promise," Fawn says and chuckles lightly.

She rushes down the stairs and takes my hand. I go with her through a long hallway lit by sconces holding candles. The hallway leads to the back of the house where there's a large kitchen. Dinner for two is already set on a large wooden table. I see berries, breads, and creams.

"Have you eaten meat since you've come back from that world?"

Actually, and even surprisingly, my answer is, "No. No, I haven't." I haven't even had a craving for meat or coffee.

"Did you eat from the trees?"

"Yeah, I did."

Fawn nods and moves to the table. I follow her. We both sit.

"Once you've eaten the food from there, it's hard to eat the food from here."

"When you say 'there,' do you mean Enu?"

"No," she whispers, "never say it here on Earth. You never know who could be listening."

"But I already told Baron about it."

"I know," she muses and looks away. "You mustn't let Felix know that. He wouldn't like it much."

"So you know my father?" I'm on the edge of my seat.

She shoves a hand toward the food. "Please, eat. You need your strength."

She's right. I'm famished because since I've returned from Enu, every time I've thought about eating a nice steak or something like my regular breakfast sandwich, I want to gag. The spread before me titillates my taste buds. As I did in Enu, I split the bread in half and spread the cream over it then pile the berries on top. It looks as though Fawn is waiting for me to take my first bite, so I eat.

"Good?" she asks while I chew.

I nod. It tastes just as divine as it did in Enu.

"Ten thousand years ago, a woman mated with an angel," she says out of the blue.

I'm caught off guard but happy about where this conversation appears to be going. "Wait." I cut her off because although I'm not religious, I read up on angels during a course on religion in under-grad. "I thought angels had no will outside of the will of God—good angels, at least."

She smiles. "You've studied. Of course you would. Your powers are rooted deep in the mind."

I take a mental note to ask her very soon what exactly that means. "Well, not on my own. I took a class."

"But you had to choose that class, right?"

"I guess so." I can already tell that Fawn is a very optimistic person.

"Just like you chose to go listen to Lario Exgesis speak."

"Who's that?" I'm completely confused.

"God, the first and last artist?" she says to jar my memory.

"You mean Dr. Dove?"

"No, I mean Lario."

"So that guy in there is not Dr. Dove; he's Lario Exgesis?"

"That will be correct," she says with a smile.

"Oh." My mind races as I wonder what the hell that was all about then. The flyer that caught my attention. The fog that rolled in and interrupted my plans to go home. And then Baron.

She chuckles. "Are you thinking?"

"I do that a lot."

"That's one of the reasons he finds you so striking. You not only have brawn but zero amounts of air in the brain." She lifts her eyebrows. "I guess our brains are more appealing after all."

We both laugh quietly.

"I apologize for interrupting you," I say. "You were saying about the angels?"

"Yes. You're right about their will. Lario and I think the mating of the angel and the woman *was* the will of God. There wasn't natural, physical sex involved in the merging. He implanted her with his seed and another seed from a place called Hope."

"So that means we're one part Hope, one part human, and one part…" *What do you call a part from an angel?*

"Divine."

"Wow," I barely say. I take a moment to reflect. "So what did this woman have? A boy or a girl?"

"A boy. And if his first breaths were to be taken here on Earth, then he would've died. So he had to be born in that place called Hope. He is the beginning of who we are."

Now I'm extremely curious about this boy. "Well, how long ago was this?"

"Around 5000 BC."

"Well, a man can't procreate alone."

"The female creature he made a vow to is

named Crystalline in our American English tongue, Ce'lah'ime in the other tongue," she says.

"You said, '*is*.' Does that mean she's still alive?"

"She'll never die."

"Okay, we have the angel and the woman and then the offspring and his—*wife*," I list.

"Not wife—mate."

"Okay, mate," I amend. "And the offspring and mate are not from here, meaning the earth?"

"So far, so right…"

"If the mate is still alive, is the offspring still alive?"

"He is."

My heart sinks. I've already come to a conclusion, and it's preposterous. It can't be! I blink and steady my breaths. "Can you tell me more about this offspring?"

"This is what Lario and I think. We know he had seven daughters with Ce'lah'ime. We think that they should be for the earth unless by their own will they choose Hope, so she couldn't keep them. As you already know, she cannot survive on the earth because she's from that place. So he watches over their seven girls until they choose to return to Crystalline."

"Is this what you *think* or know?" I ask.

"It's what we think."

"And this boy, it's Felix, isn't it?"

"It's Felix," she confirms.

"He's your father too?"

"We're sisters."

I'm dizzy now. I think she can feel it, because she takes my hand. I'm instantly calmed.

"But Felix is way darker than you," I say.

"It's not strange at all, Cl'auta. The tribes of this earth were the products of three brothers. But color has become a human limitation, and we are less human than all the other parts of us. Haven't you felt it all of your life?"

"I have," I whisper.

"Would you like to stop for the night? We can continue tomorrow."

"No," I quickly answer, wanting to learn more. "Adore said… Wait, have you met Adore?"

"I don't think so." She ruffles her eyebrows as though she's trying to remember. "But I have heard of her."

"She wouldn't tell me who she was. Who is she?"

"I think she's the first daughter."

My mouth falls open. "My goodness. She can't be that old. She looks, well, our age!"

"You didn't want to leave her, did you?"

"No, I didn't. I don't want to leave you either."

She nods. "I know. This desire keeps us close. We'll always need each other."

I study Fawn's face. Though we look exactly the same age, she's way more seasoned than I am. "How old are you?"

"Three hundred and twenty-five years old, I believe."

"You don't know?"

She looks off. I notice that some of Fawn's memories, those regarding herself, seem hidden behind a wall.

But still, shock has knocked the breath out of me.

"I know," she says with a reassuring smile. "I've adjusted to the history of the human race, but it hasn't been easy. I only arrived to this country sixty years ago. Then ten years later, Glo was born, and then twenty years later, you were born. Our mother gave up her last of seven seeds fourteen years ago with Zillael. She was named after Felix's mother, who lived near a waterfall of the Great River. Zillael, our sister, is the only one of us with a pure human name that has no translation.

"Like I said, it was around 5000 BC when

Zillael, our grandmother, met the angel and left the earth for that place called Hope. She could only survive there because of the child she carried. Once he was born, she…"

"Died," I finish.

"Yes. When Felix was old enough, he returned her remains to the waterfall and buried her there. It was after the flood."

"You mean *the* flood?"

"Forty days and forty nights of rain."

"Wow." I sit back in my seat, attempting to bear the weight of what's been revealed to me. If we're divine, then I wonder why God went through all of that trouble just to create us.

"Lario was once a vampire too," she says.

"But he's human!"

"He was born human and then was seduced by a Selell and made a vampire. Now he's a man again."

I want to choke off the surprise this newest revelation has caused. If Baron could be human again, then we could live happily ever after as a normal couple.

She hears me thinking that and says, "They won't ever stop hunting you, Clarity, even if your lover is a man. They won't stop until you're dead and your blood has been consumed by the fittest."

"But don't I have to be alive for vampires to be able to drink my blood? I mean, that's how it is in horror movies."

"This is no horror movie, Cl'auta. This is real life, and your blood is Life Blood—dead or alive."

"Well, that's disturbing."

"That's why we live out here. We can see someone coming a mile away. Sometimes they'll send a human to attack us, but if I can see them coming, then I can push them back."

The tray that holds the bread, cream, and berries goes flying across the table and then back in front of us without even a single berry disturbed. I stare at Fawn in awe. I'm falling deeper and deeper down the rabbit hole. I know this will never be over.

"I wanted to be a teacher," I confess out of the blue. "Live in a small town. A cottage with a stream nearby and have a gazebo with a wooden swing to watch the sunset after a perfect day."

Fawn smiles at me. "I put a lot on your mind tonight, didn't I?"

"It's been pretty heavy."

"I know, but I have to tell you this. We have a lot

to do before you can get your cottage and stream and become a teacher."

"Are you saying it could happen still?"

She nods, smiling. "Do you want to know how Lario became human again?"

I take a sip of tea. My eyes light up.

It's Goshem tea, she says.

But how?

Felix.

For a brief second, I wonder if Felix has been a better father to her than he has to me.

"We, with our Life Blood, have access to the Tree of Life," she says. "I was granted a leaf to restore him."

"You mean *the* Tree of Life?"

"It exists. It's guarded, as it's written, but it's here on Earth, and only *we* have access to it. Do you understand the gravity of that?"

"I'm starting to." My head is spinning. I can't believe what I'm hearing. I can't believe I, *of all people*, am special in this way. I don't know why, but I close my eyes and ask in a prayer, *Why me?*

"Maybe we can save all Selells, but they won't be patient and wait to find out because they're determined," Fawn continues.

I'm sure she didn't hear my prayer. "What do you mean by determined?"

"If they drink our blood, then not only will they be restored, they'll be more than mere human beings. They'll have your ability, and if they find the entrance to that place called Hope, they'll be able to enter it."

"That would be tragic," I say, thinking about how peaceful Enu was. "But Lario didn't drink your blood, did he?"

"No, he did not. And Ze Feldis will die before he drinks yours."

"I felt Baron's thirst, you know? It's the most agonizing feeling in the world." I swallow, remembering that aching feeling in my throat. "Could I find the Tree of Life for him?"

"You could." She takes a sip of Goshem tea. "Or we could try to save him another way, a better way."

"You said *we*?"

"You, Glo, Zillael, and I are part of a larger mystery. Lario and I can't figure it out on our own. There's a text buried deep in the earth that would help, but only the Encaser can discover it."

"And that would be me."

She sighs and falls back into her seat. "That would be you."

WE AGREE THAT IS ENOUGH TALK ABOUT THE HEFTY things in our lives. We finish eating and drink more Goshem tea. Without using words, I tell her all about my visit to Enu. I tell her about Adore and how beautiful she is, about the green grass, and how my deepest desires materialized to form my world. I tell her how Baron came to me in the window and that is why I chose to leave. I could never live in a world he's not part of.

Very early in the morning, Baron and I end up in a guest room on the top floor. I take off my pants and bra, leaving on my tank top and panties. I'd rather sleep nude, but I don't want to make things more difficult for him. He keeps his eyes off of me as I peel off my clothes. It's clear his avoidance is deliberate. The house is quite chilly, so I slide under the quilt.

He gets in behind me and wraps his arms around me. "They're pink now," he says, referring to my panties.

We both laugh. I turn to face him, and after a long time looking into my eyes, he presses his lips onto mine. Not long after, he flips me on my back and puts his hand between my thighs again. His fingers go to that spot, and before I know it, I'm moaning in deep pleasure.

"You can do it," I whisper, encouraging him to go all the way this time.

His eyes are pinned to my face, and even as I speak, he does it again. I pull his shirt up by the hem and lift it over his head. He lets me.

His chest is solid, and the ripples of muscles are flawless. The contrasting colors of our skin look like a Picasso drawn in chiaroscuro. As the explosion within me ignites, I can't help but form the expression he so desires.

He growls long and hard. "Clarity." He moves rapidly on top of and inside me.

I cannot believe what we're having is mere sex. Every thrust sparks orgasmic sensations. The pleasure is overwhelmingly divine. Baron's moans make him sound vulnerable. As our bodies merge, he's warm all over as if his skin has never been ice cold a day in his life. There's even sweat on his brow. I want to kiss him, do something besides lie here, but the pleasure is so potent that I'm lost in it. I want to thank the angel who made the first of my kind and who or whatever made the first of his kind.

"Baron," I plead, but what for, I don't know.

I see in his face that he's battling over-heightened urges. When a loud moan escapes my throat and I can no longer control my body, he lets go. His letting go is *way* more intense than mine. I'm still in a euphoric daze, but his top lip is pulled up over his front teeth and his fangs are visible. He's staring at my face, but I know he's not seeing me as a Bloody Mary cocktail. I touch his cheek, and he gently pelts my palm with kisses. Those same lips then find my mouth.

Gosh, he tastes like he smells, like crushed peaches and mint. "Baron?"

"Clarity," he whispers back.

"You have to give me a break," I say because I feel it starting over again.

Before a second passes, he's behind me with his arms wrapped around me. I love how all I have to do is mention my will, and without hesitation, he obliges. His deeper desire is to keep me happy.

I want to know why sex with him is this way. Why don't I have to build up to the blast? Why is *it* there from the moment we start? Before I can ask, Baron is actually asleep. His hold on me has not loosened, and I let myself fall asleep in his arms.

CHAPTER

TWENTY-THREE

I t's probably around noon when I wake up, but the room is dark because there aren't any windows. Baron is still asleep. I pry myself out of his arms, slide off the bed, fumble around in the dark to get dressed, and tiptoe out of the bedroom. When I get downstairs, Fawn and Lario are at the table. They study my sheepish grin.

"You look twice as radiant this morning," Fawn says.

I sniff a bashful chuckle. "I slept very well."

"And Ze Feldis is asleep?" Lario's tone is highly curious.

"I believe so—or is he dead for the moment?"

They laugh.

"In folklore, vampires sleep during the daylight

in crypts, but in real life, they're lethargic all the time. The thirst aches so much that they can't sleep. But something about you soothes Ze Feldis's thirst. Interesting…" he says.

"Your bath is through there and up the stairs." Fawn thumbs over her shoulder. "We're having Goshem tea at the moment, but when you return, we'll eat."

I nod and go in the direction she pointed. The bathroom is relaxing. It contains a single whirlpool tub and a window. As I rest in the warm water, my body remembers what Baron did to it not so long ago. He's already becoming an addiction. I remember his kisses and his hand sliding up my thigh. I remember how fast he entered me, how needy for me he was. Then my stomach growls, and I realize that he drained every ounce of energy out of me. I'm craving berries, cream, and Goshem tea.

I step out of the tub and wrap a towel around me. I happen to glance out the window and see a striking dark man wearing black, his blue eyes glowing, moving across the grass. His steps are hard, deliberate, and he's moving very fast. I put clothes on as fast as I can. While buttoning my jeans, I race downstairs and run to the front door.

Viesel Egos doesn't even ring the doorbell.

Once I get to the bottom of the stairs, the door flies open, and he grabs my arm, pulling on me.

"Let's go," he demands.

"What are you doing?" I struggle against his grip, but he's too strong.

I don't have to fight for long because Baron is here. In an instant, I'm released, and he and Viesel Egos fight again.

Baron tosses Viesel Egos into a bookcase, and an avalanche of books rain down on him. Like an arrow on fire, Viesel comes shooting out of the stacks as Fawn and Lario rush into the living room. Viesel pulls a flaming sword from one of his pockets and takes a swing at Baron, who shifts just in time to avoid the blade. Viesel recovers quickly and takes another swipe at him. This time, it catches Baron across the shoulder and slices him.

Tell him to stop, Fawn shouts in my head.

"Stop, Viesel Egos, stop," I scream.

Just like that, Viesel Egos's sword is disengaged. He makes one backward move and ends up standing on the threshold of the doorway. Baron is a few feet away from him, avoiding the direct sunlight. The men glare at each other, looking as if they would happily rumble again at any second.

The shallow cut on Baron's shoulder is already healing. I'm relieved about that.

"Are you insane?" I shout at Viesel Egos.

"This is a dangerous place. Let's go." He hasn't taken his eyes off Baron yet.

"She's with me. She's safe," Baron says.

"It's because of you she's not safe. You're a vampire."

"I love her."

"I'm her guardian. I've been killing your kind all night."

Then almost out of reflex, Viesel Egos looks at Fawn. His eyes go from Fawn, to me, and back to Fawn. He frowns harder than usual until he sees Lario. He's instantly taken aback by the sight of him. "Exgesis?"

Lario steps forward. "Egos."

Viesel Egos carefully walks over to Lario and sniffs at him. "You're human."

"I'm human."

"But how?"

"I ate a leaf from the Tree of Life."

Viesel stares at Fawn with condemnation in his eyes, but that condemnation could always be there. I see Fawn nod, and I know he said something to her.

Fawn's eyes race toward me. I hear her say, *Encase me.*

I do so, and I see myself watching Fawn. Baron narrows his eyes at us.

Both of you are not safe here, Viesel Egos wastes no time telling us. *My oath is to protect the Life Blood of Cl'auta. I have also sworn an oath to protect the Life Blood of the house of Benel of Felix. If you do not want to see the blood of Ze Feldis and Exgesis spilled, then you must leave with me.*

"No," she says.

Viesel Egos wastes no time engaging his sword. He glares at Lario and Baron like a mad bull staring down a red cloak. Fawn aims her palm at him, and he goes flying out the door into the daylight. Baron rushes over and places his arms around my body, but he lets go right away. He knows I am not there.

Viesel Egos is back in the doorway, his eyes glowing brighter than usual. He's ready to fight. I cannot encase him—because he's my guardian, I presume—but I can persuade him. I'll have to make it quick because we haven't got long before all hell breaks loose. I let go of Fawn as a whole.

"Viesel Egos," I say when I'm back in my body. "What are you going to do? Kill all of us?"

"I'm going to start with the new human and end with the vampire."

"Does that mean you think you're above God?" I ask.

Deep contemplation crosses Viesel Egos's face. I've got him thinking, and that's exactly the pause I need.

"If God created us and the Tree of Life, and if Lario ate the leaf and lived, then by whose will is he standing here?" I ask.

"His own," Viesel Egos says with a snarl.

That wasn't the answer I was looking for, but I go with it. "Exactly."

Baron puts his arms around me again. One side of Viesel Egos's lip twitches, but he stands down by disengaging his sword.

"And what about the other vampires who want to be human again?" I ask. "If they can be changed back and we can help them, then shouldn't we try?" I'm all out of words. My argument, though weak, is on the table for him to accept or reject.

"All you have to do is tell him to get out of here, Clarity. He has to obey you," Baron says through a snarl.

I shake my head. "No, I won't tell him that. I will ask you, Viesel Egos, to help us—please?"

Baron's growl reverberates in my ear. I'm sure he's already counted this as the third time Viesel Egos has used a blade on him. The same hate shines in his adversary's eyes.

"I'll be there when you need me," are Viesel's final words. He backs out of the house, and the door slams shut.

———

At first we're all silent. Nothing moves until in one full gush, the massive bookcase is back against the wall with all the books back in place.

"And that's in alphabetical order, right, sweetie?" Lario says to Fawn with a wink. He's obviously trying to lighten the mood.

"Of course," she says, going along with his plan.

Lario walks over to the stacks. "Good, now the vampire can go upstairs and put on a shirt, and we can get to work."

Baron uses his lightning speed to face me. He stares into my eyes for a long moment before disappearing upstairs. I look at Fawn, who's standing at the bookcase watching me. We both know he's in a foul mood.

That's a vampire for you. He must really want to kill the guardian, but he loves you more, she says.

Could a vampire kill the guardian? I ask her. All three times, Viesel's gotten the best of Baron.

"You see I'm without one," Fawn says.

Lario glances at us from the top of a ladder that's pushed against the bookshelf. "Ah, a conversation between sisters, I see." He slides a book off the shelf. "Ze Feldis and I will have to have our own tête-à-tête between vampires. Oh, wait, I can't, because I'm only the guy who almost got his head chopped off by a psychotic guardian. By the way, thank you for saving his life, Clarity. My lady here was going to make a natural disaster out of him."

I wonder when he'll get serious.

He studies my perplexed expression and shouts, "Finally, the perfect match for Ze Feldis! A prudent woman." Lario holds a book toward me. "You'll need this."

"What's this?" I ask with a bite. My mind is still heavy. I want this all to be over with, but I know we're only at the beginning.

"I must confess there are things I miss about being a vampire, like never having to crawl up this thing." He looks down at the ladder he's standing on.

"Just give her the book," Fawn says. The book flies out of his hand and into mine. "He was worse as a vampire."

I sniff a chuckle at that, forcing myself to be amused. "Sorry to be Debbie Downer, it takes me a while to wind down. That's why I rarely wind up." The title of the book grabs all of my attention: *The Bloods of Life?* It's written in a very strange language.

"You can read it!" Lario moves down the ladder. "I've been trying to crack that language for years—seven years, three months, six hours, and"—he twists his wrist to study the face of his watch—"thirty-three minutes, to be exact."

I flip the cover open. "I need a pen and note-book." I walk over to the sofa and sit. Out of nowhere, both tools fly over to me.

"Thanks, Fawn, I can really get used to this," I joke, hoping to prove I'm not so serious all the time. The truth is, I actually am a very serious person, or being, or whatever I am.

But both Fawn and Lario chuckle, so it must've worked.

HOURS PASS, AND I'M STILL CAPTIVATED BY THE book. I translate as I go. Before now, my ability to understand any language has frightened me. Like so many other things about myself, I viewed my ability as another handicap, and I tried to stay away from those who spoke a language other than English and Spanish. I didn't want to face the fact that I could comprehend their tongue without ever studying it.

The text contains more information about my grandmother, Zillael. It calls her *the bearer of the seed*. She arrived at the falls during a drought to send up a prayer to the Creator. Not many walked in the way of the Creator still, and Zillael believed they were being punished for it. She prayed to the one who'd created the lands, waters, and air and cried for mercy. Tears as thick as hail rolled from her eyes, and when she saw a man standing before her, she became fearful.

He told her, "No fear." He explained that her prayer had been answered, and he touched her forehead.

Then she saw how evil man had become gods to themselves with no regard for human life. She saw water pour down and drown the souls. Instead of begging for mercy, they cursed the Creator. Zillael's heart ached. Unable to see any more of the future, she pulled his hand from her forehead and pleaded for the lives of humans, offering her own life as a sacrifice for many.

"Who are you but a mere human?" the angel asked.

"I am nothing but the daughter of Halkah, the great man and poor soul, deserter of the one true God."

The angel said her request had been heard, accepted, and granted. She fell into a deep sleep and woke up in Enu.

By the time I decipher this much of the text, night had fallen again. I read my notes to Lario and Fawn.

"Finally, a tiny bit more comprehension," Lario shouts dramatically as we sit at the table eating dinner. He picks up a blueberry and rolls it between his fingers. "Did you know that before the flood, humans were only granted the consumption of fruit and vegetables, which included the herb?"

"No," Fawn says as I say, "Yes."

"It may explain the berry craving you ladies have."

"Maybe..." I glance over my shoulder. "You would think he would've calmed down by now." I catch Fawn and Lario staring at each other, and I'm instantly alarmed. "What?"

"Ze Feldis is not here," Lario says.

"What?" I shoot to my feet. "Where is he?"

Fawn stands too. "He left early this afternoon."

"Where did he go, and why didn't you tell me?"

"I'm sorry," Fawn says. "It was something Viesel Egos said to him."

I try to remember everything Viesel said this afternoon. Other than the standard "He's a vampire who wants to kill you" bit, which we both know will never happen, what could have sent him away?

"Whatever Viesel Egos said, he said only to Ze Feldis," Fawn says after reading my thoughts.

I rush to the front door, Fawn and Lario right behind me. I swing it open and look way across the thorny grass field to the dark tree line. When I look harder, I see flashes of light and hear faint cries of agony.

"It's Viesel Egos," Fawn says as she wraps her arms around me. Her grasp is soothing.

I know I can't go out there. I'm not built to fight in that way. "Don't you have protection here?"

"Felix knows I can protect us with my power, even if it's exhausting. He thinks once I get tired of being on the lookout all the time, I'll do what he wants."

I frown. That doesn't sound like Felix at all. "Does he want you to leave Lario?"

"Our father didn't approve of my asking for a leaf off the Tree of Life. He said it was dangerous, and I could've been killed."

"But you weren't."

Then an idea comes to me. I close my eyes and think of the car parked along the side of the road. To my surprise, it's still there. I take from the energy surrounding it and spread as much as I can over the house and at least fifteen miles around us. When I open my eyes, the flashes in the woods have stopped.

Fawn lets go of me and looks up in all directions. "You did it!" She runs out into the yard and skips around the lawn. "The amazing protective covering!"

"I don't know why I didn't think of it earlier."

I'm happy to see her happy, and by the glint in Lario's eyes, he is too.

"He went after Zina," he says to me, still beaming at Fawn, who's skipping freely all over the yard.

I nod. I'm still caught in my initial reaction to

Baron leaving without telling me, and I'm clueless to understand what that reaction is—anger, grief, fear, and understanding all wrapped up into one.

We spend the night outside, beside a bonfire Lario built, combing over the rest of the book and drinking Goshem tea. We sit on cushiony lounge chairs that were dusty until Fawn stirred up a wind that knocked the dust out of them.

"We know all about Zillael's short life in that place called Hope, so skip over that part," Lario says and flops a hand dismissively.

"We can say it now, right?" Fawn asks Lario specifically. "There's protection."

He hesitates and says, "Why, yes, I guess so."

Fawn's face lights up. "Enu—that place is called Enu." We smile at each other.

"I've been thinking…" Lario sets his chin on his thumb and scratches the side of his face.

"Yes?" Fawn says.

"The *Book of the Seven Seeds*. Do you think they're buried with her?"

"Who?" Fawn and I ask at the same time.

"Surely you're asking me this for effect," he says.

Fawn rolls her eyes and winks at me. "He's testy sometimes. Yes, darling." She leans over in her chair toward him. "We already know the answer, but we still want to hear it from you."

That's when I burst out laughing, mainly because it's so true—and she's so sarcastic about it. My laughter is infectious because Fawn bursts into laughter too. Eventually so does Lario, and we can't stop.

I wonder what she's laughing about. I'm laughing at the fact that all of this is actually true. There's actually a book in my hand about a woman who lived thousands of years ago—and she's my *grandmother*. Not my great-great-great-great—and way more greats—grandmother but my actual paternal *grandmother*. This woman was approached by an angel, impregnated, and taken to a crazy place where I saw *pink* and *silver* trees. I'm laughing because my mother, who was not such a very good mother, is not my mother, and if she's my guardian, then maybe she sucked at that too. My father, who is my father, has seven children, all girls, and he too is thousands of years old. I mean—*thousands*.

I'm also laughing because sex with Baron, my vampire lover, was unreal, and he's gone off to challenge the scary little vampire witch who had him stuck in a cave and drained his energy. Could the twists of life get any more comical? I think not.

That's why I laugh louder and harder until I'm curled up in a ball, wiping tears from my eyes and sniffing them back. To my surprise, so is Fawn.

Lario just looks at us, shaking his head as he takes the book from me. "Okay, no more reading for you two tonight—we'll continue tomorrow." He heads to the door. "Carry on." He disappears inside.

Fawn and I calm down about twenty minutes later. We hiccup restrained giggles as we slump in our seats and study the fire.

"I'm glad you're here," she says after a long period of silence.

"Me too." I stretch out my arm toward her.

She takes my hand, and we watch the blaze, talking all night about all the things I wanted to say to someone when I was a child, growing up in my wacky home.

I don't remember when I fall asleep, but the sun is up when I open my eyes. Fawn and I have thick quilts over us, the fire is out, and a beautiful dark man with ice-blue eyes bears down over me.

"Viesel Egos," I mutter, trying to blink him into focus.

"You took from the car? You were not supposed to do that" are the first words out of his mouth.

"And good morning to you too." I pull the quilt up to my neck. Lario must've spread them over us after we fell asleep.

Viesel Egos just stands there, giving me a look of disapproval and expectation.

"But I'm glad you're here," I whisper. "I was thinking last night that you know where Felix is, and I need to speak to him."

To my surprise, he nods and says, "I'll take you to him."

"Us?"

"Not the vampire."

"You mean the man? The human being? The only vampire that was here is gone because of something you said to him."

Viesel just stares at me.

I sit up to stretch my back. "Well, he has to come with us. Fawn and I need to see our father, and Lario is Fawn's partner, so he goes where she goes."

Just like that, Viesel becomes a shadow moving across the grass and into the trees. Fawn, who's been playing possum, opens her eyes and looks at me.

"That was a strange reply," I say.

She sits up and drops the quilt to her lap. "I

didn't tell you, but Lario is the one who killed my 'Viesel Egos.'"

"He did?" I stupidly ask. Of course he did—she just told me.

"He was only protecting himself. But you know Viesel's kind have no love for vampires—or human beings, for that matter. I don't even think they like us too much. He's just doing his job—that's all."

I gaze off toward the trees again. I hide my thoughts from Fawn because somehow, I don't think she's right. "I understand," I tell her. "Are you ready to go in? I can't believe we slept out here all night."

"It's having protection. It's so comforting."

We wrap ourselves in our quilts and head inside. Fawn shows me to a guest room with a window and no memories of making love to Baron. I can't believe he left me alone like this. My heart is broken, but at the same time, all of this new knowledge energizes me. We have a purpose—a life-altering one. Plus, I have two sisters in this world that I've never met, Glo and Zilleal. I hope their lives aren't as lonely as mine was before I met Adore and Fawn. I can't imagine life without either of them now. Relying on skyscrapers for companionship and the sounds of the city for conversation seems like ages ago.

After I bathe, we eat and resume digging into the book. All three of us sit in the living room, trying to find any new answers that will lead us toward a purpose the seven sisters may have. To speed up the process, I go right to the end, where there's a chart of etchings that appear to be hieroglyphic symbols.

"I think it's a map," I say. "By the way, Lario, where did you get this book?"

"I didn't," he answers, frowning at the page as if whatever he's reading is working his brain. "Fawn stole it."

I look at her for an answer.

She continues reading as she says, "No, I didn't. It just followed me out of Vatican City. Those hoards."

I snort and shake my head. She glances at me, grinning.

"So this other book that we need to find didn't follow you out as well?" I ask.

"It wasn't there, but if it had been, then I'm sure it would've."

I smirk at her. "You know that makes you an international criminal?"

"Amongst other things," Lario adds.

Finally, I hold the book open at the last page

and sigh. "Well, I think Lario's right. The book may be wherever Zillael is buried. I'm thinking that's where this map leads. Because up here"—I run my finger across a sentence at the top of the page—"it reads, and I'm putting the English spin on it, 'and we return her to the mark of her people.' That mark means the place where remains mark the earth. At least, that's the context it's being used in throughout the book."

"Felix buried her, we think," Fawn says.

"I can try to find him with or without Viesel's help," I say.

"Then what?"

"We pay our father a visit."

"And then what?" she asks.

"I think I can convince him to tell us where her gravesite is."

Fawn gives a look that says she thinks I'm out of my mind. But I can work Felix; I know I can.

She must hear what I'm thinking, because she says, "Are we talking about the same Felix?"

"What other choice do we have?"

The looks on all of our faces answer that question. We have to find Felix no matter how fruitless our efforts may prove to be.

CHAPTER

TWENTY-FOUR

F awn, Lario, and I are sitting on the sofas in what I now know they call the reading room, not the living room. Lario explained that they have no set room to *live* in; they *live* in each one of them, "so what does living room actually mean?"

It took me a while to crack a slight smile at that. I was trying to figure out what I thought of his proclamation—the word *high-minded* came to mind. Something about Lario irritates me slightly. I think if he weren't hooked up with Fawn and I'd met him in my old life, I probably wouldn't have anything to say to him beyond customary salutations.

It's difficult to recall the energy of a man who has always been so scarce in my life, but I'm trying. I'm sweating and straining, attempting to reach Felix anywhere on the face of this earth. Two hours have gone by. My head feels as if it's on the verge of exploding, and my eyes are smashed together so tight, I think my lids are going to merge into each other.

"Stop," Fawn cries, grabbing my shoulders. "Stop before you hurt yourself."

I open my eyes, panting. My mind can't let it go. I wonder why Felix could contact me in the taxicab in Dallas, but I can't reach him now.

"I'll make you some tea," Fawn says before rushing off to the kitchen.

I look at Lario, who's studying me intensely.

"How do you feel?" he asks.

"Fine," I say. "I think we have to go out and find him."

"Hey, I'm with you," Lario says, holding up his hands in surrender.

"Good." My tone solidifies our plan.

Fawn returns with the tea. She hands me a cup and sits back down with her own cup.

"We can start in New York," I continue. "I think if Fawn and I combine our abilities, we can handle just about anything."

I see Fawn turn stiff.

Lario looks at her. "We can't sit here combing through books forever, sweetheart."

I hear and feel Fawn's dread. She's not afraid for herself; she's afraid for Lario. Her connection to him seems very strong, but I can't get a read on Lario even if I try. I wonder why.

"Maybe just you and I can go," I say in an attempt to soothe her.

"Oh, no, you two aren't having all the fun," Lario says, wiggling his finger at us.

I look at Fawn for the final word. She nods with a tired sigh.

THE WOODS ARE DEAD SILENT. ALL THAT CAN BE heard are our steps smashing against the twigs, weeds, and vines. Something flies above our heads, some sort of shadow. I look up. It looks like a very large cutout of a blackbird, but then it isn't, because it doesn't have an exact form.

"What is that?" I ask.

"It's *the evil*," Lario answers.

"Yes, I remember that very well," I say.

"It's always on the search. Usually if there's protection, then there's something to kill nearby."

"But how can it kill us, and why does it want to?"

"It wants the creatures in this world, like vampires, to stay what they are. It will obliterate anything it's created to keep it that way. Its goal is to maintain the status quo."

"When you say 'anything it's created,' do you mean there are more than vampires out there?"

"Absolutely!" he says so loudly that the word echoes in the woods.

"Shush," Fawn warns him.

I ponder how insane that sounds. "So you're saying there are werewolves and zombies and other monsters that go bump in the night?"

"Close," Lario sings, too cheerful for the subject matter. He takes off ahead of us.

I watch his back, masking my new opinion of him. I think he's a tad cavalier. I do want to know more though, and he seems to love being the bearer of information. "What do you mean, close? Are you saying people can turn into animals? And a wolf, in particular?" I stop in my tracks to wait for an answer.

"Don't stop walking," Fawn instructs as she continues forward. She glances up at the shadowy figure that just flew over us. She's frightened out of her mind.

"If humans get mixed up in enough darkness, then anything is possible, even transforming into a wolf," Lario answers.

I shake my head as I move forward. What drives a person to want to get involved with this evil?

"But don't worry," Lario continues. "Contrary to popular belief, absolutely none of it can harm human beings unless they invite it in. Though it's quite unfortunate that people invite them in, mostly willingly and frequently ignorantly."

The car is not far away, and I'm happy for that. Fawn keeps checking over her shoulders and above us. I don't think she trusts the protection as much as I do. I move up beside her and take her hand. She squeezes my hand back. As soon as we see the car, I dig for the keys in my bag.

Fawn unlocks the doors with her mind. "Sorry, you're taking too long."

"No problem." I toss the keys to Lario. "I guess you'll drive, and we'll stay on the lookout."

"Nothing's better than a woman with a plan," he says and slides into the driver's seat.

I take the backseat, and Fawn gets into the

passenger's seat. Lario backs up, making the tires screech, and cuts a sharp U-turn, and we're off.

"The address is—"

"PH3600 Madison Avenue," Fawn finishes for me. "I've been there."

I nod and twist in my seat to stare out of the rear window. I can no longer see the shadow. I look out the side windows. It's not following us as it did the day I entered Enu. The woods look clear of any danger. I observe little details that went unnoticed on the drive up here.

A road about two miles south and off the right leads to a place called Bob's Apple Orchard and a town called Blue Star Bay. If we were just an average family taking a normal trip, then I'd ask Lario to turn off so we could pick apples and tour the town with the cute name.

I think of Baron and wonder how he's doing. I also wonder how he could leave me. Maybe I am wrong and he doesn't love me. Even as a human, Lario can't stand to be away from Fawn. I lean my head back and close my eyes to toy with the idea of finding Baron. I open my eyes, and Fawn is facing me.

"Go ahead and get some rest. I'll watch," she says.

I close my eyes and recall the last time I was with Baron. He's standing behind me, and even while facing down the beautiful, destroying angel named Viesel Egos, I want to melt in Baron's grasp. I don't even have to remember seeing him with his shirt off or how we made love for the first time. That mental image of him is enough to take me to him.

The place looks like an underground sewer. The stench stings my nose and rattles my brain. It's like urine mixed with animal carcasses. Constant water droplets echo in the background. Thank goodness I'm not actually standing in the shallow layer of stale water that's spread over the moldy concrete. I hear footsteps pounding the cement and splashing the water, and I find a crevice to hide in.

In only a few seconds, seven male figures, one in the middle and three on each side of him, plus one female stomp by. The one in the center is Baron, who I'm sure doesn't see me. He snaps his face in the opposite direction though, which may indicate that he senses my nearness. I have to be cautious.

Dust and grime at least two inches thick on the cement wall in front of me is the only reason I shoot out of the crevice. I see others in the tunnel. One guy has his teeth sunk into a girl's neck. She looks to be seventeen or eighteen. Her eyes are wide open and seem to stare at me before they roll up. He lets go of her when he's done, and she collapses. Then he leaves.

In my bodiless state, I rush over to her and put two invisible fingers against her neck to check for a pulse. She's dead, and my heart sinks. Killing her happened so fast; it seemed too easy. I look around to get a hint of where I am. The abandoned train tracks and chained doors indicate that we're beneath some borough in New York.

Baron and the six others kick down one of those chained doors and flow into a lightless space. I'm torn between staying with the girl's body and moving on with my mission. There's nothing I can do for her, so I pass a guy who's flicking a lighter off and on, entranced by the fire, and three figures making out in one of those crevices.

I move to the doorway and peek around the corner. Five steps lead down to a tight chamber where flickers of firelight beat against the walls. It's faint, but I hear voices. One by one, I descend the steps. I get to the edge of the opening of the room. I try so hard not to touch the walls that in the moment, I forget to avoid the filth and part of my body goes right through it.

"I'm not your prisoner," Baron growls.

He sounds strong, not broken, and I sigh with relief because of that.

"Only if you could take us all on," one of the male vampires says.

I can't see him, but I can imagine his face when he says, "The hell I can't."

There's laughter; clearly they're mocking him.

"Where is she?" another male asks.

I need to see their faces, so I move through the cement. When I step out of the wall, I've missed a portion of the conversation. I'm *in* the room, and if Baron turns and looks behind him, he'll see me. The six guys are clearly vampires. They're very pale, and their faces are hard, intense. I notice their eyes are shifty, cautiously keeping tabs on the next person. There's danger in the air.

The one with jet-black hair and glassy black eyes leans toward Baron. "Is she telling the truth? You've bonded with her." His voice booms in the tight space.

"I barely even know her," Baron says with a growl.

"He's lying! I saw her when…" Zina stops short of confessing.

"When what?" Baron presses. "Do you want to

tell your band of allies how you stabbed me with silver daggers and hid me in a tomb? Just so you can have the Life Blood for yourself. She wanted to drink it all, and she still does."

In a flash, Zina's up in his face. The tips of their noses are almost touching, but Baron doesn't flinch.

"I did not stick you in a tomb. It was a cave," she says.

His expression remains even. "Try it again, and you'll be headless."

A low growl rumbles in her throat but not his.

"Don't you love me anymore, Ze Feldis?" Her tone has changed. It's seductive. She opens her legs, slides onto his lap, and slides her tongue up his neck.

It makes my stomach sour, but I force myself to be strong as I get a good look at her. Zina has silky jet-black hair, pale skin, and crystal blue eyes. Her features are sharp. She's a perfect, exotic temptress. The good thing is, she's not on Baron's lap for long. One of the men in the room grabs her by the back of the neck and tosses her right through me. I feel the hollowness of her soul surrounding me, like being trapped in a freezing cold prison. When she drops to her feet, I'm glad I'm no longer confined inside her.

"I think you're playing us," the vampire roars. "We don't need you. We have who we want right here." He glares at Baron.

"She's here," Zina shouts and turns to the wall, not quite seeing me but looking my way.

Without warning, Baron is on his feet, wielding two daggers. He twists and turns, taking the blade to the men in the room so fast, all I see is blood spattering and heads flying. Zina flies out of the room while he's engaged, and I know she got away because of me.

When all six men are headless—and in a few cases armless—Baron whips around to glare at me. He's never looked at me in that way. Instead of facing his wrath, I open my eyes.

TWENTY-FIVE

I return to myself. I can't stop myself from balling up and whimpering.

Fawn reaches for my hand. "Are you okay?"

I take her hand and nod. I can't speak, but if I can cry for a little while, I think I'll be okay. Reading my mind, she lets go of my hand and leaves me alone with my heartache.

Highway I-20 is jam-packed going through Hartford, and my tears just won't stop falling. That look he gave me is etched in my memory. How could he go from loving me to hating me? Maybe Viesel Egos was right; in the end, he's a vampire. But I know that Baron is comforting and patient and caring, at least toward me. I haven't seen a dark side of him, even as he chopped the heads off other vampires. Thus, I'm confused.

Suddenly, the car comes to a grinding halt. Even with my seat belt on, I bang into the back of the driver's seat.

"What in the world?" I mutter, looking around.

A white pickup truck has stopped in front of us. I look to my right and see a red Toyota Tercel that's stopped, and to the left is a big gray SUV.

"They're boxing us in," Lario shouts.

Not only have the three drivers gotten out of their cars, but more drivers have stopped, exited their vehicles, and are heading our way.

I'm too curious to be afraid. Maybe I'm still asleep after returning from the Red Yard event, and this isn't happening. However, when the first tire iron smashes the back window and I duck to protect myself from the glass that rains down on me, I know I'm wide awake. Before the guy with the tire iron can take a second swing, he flies across the highway.

Fawn's face is tormented. "I don't want to hurt them."

"Well, it's either them or us," Lario shouts,

ducking from an assault on the driver's-side window with what looks like a cardboard coffee cup.

This is insane! All four tires are slashed, and the car lowers. The guy in the SUV has what looks like a shotgun, and he racks it. Without hesitation, I encasc him, make him unload the rifle, and throw it away. When I'm back inside me, I feel for the protection, but it's gone.

We're unprotected, and I wonder how I missed that. All of our windows are being smashed out, and things like cans, cups, and anything else that can be picked up and thrown are hitting the car.

"Fawn," Lario shouts, "do it before we end up dead!"

I can see how conflicted she is. Her power is so forceful, and mine is intrusive in a less aggressive way. I close my eyes to try something. I push myself out into space rather than into a vessel. It's heavier and takes way more concentration. I have to repeat what I want to fill this space over and over again. The only word I can come up with is peace.

I'm not sure if it's working or not, but the car has stopped shaking and the glass has stopped shattering. I'm still pushing. I'm not sure how far I have to go. It's not until I hear a familiar voice command us to get out of the car that I open my eyes.

Viesel Egos stands at my door. I let go of the veil of peace. Everyone is a bit woozy at first, but then the mayhem begins again. Viesel Egos isn't as temperate as Fawn or me. Bodies fly everywhere, and so do the cars, as he clears space.

"Let's move," Viesel almost shouts.

We all hurry out of the car and follow him. As Viesel swings his arm, objects fly backward. People are crying; cars and trucks are landing on them. Viesel's black Town Car is parked along the side of the road. The doors shoot open, and Fawn, Lario, and I file into the backseat. As soon as we're in, the doors slam shut. Viesel Egos slams the car into reverse and speeds backward. I look behind us as Viesel Egos weaves through the open paths, not hitting anyone or anything. I'm quite sure people don't even see his car passing by, and if any part of the vehicle gets close enough to hit someone, a force flings the person out of the way.

"Where do you think you were going?" Viesel Egos barks.

I look at the rearview mirror. Those glowing eyes are trained on me, waiting for an answer. My eyes are wide. I can't believe he wants to have this conversation *now*.

"To see Felix," I say.

"I told you to wait."

"You didn't tell me anything."

I grab the door handle as Viesel backs the car off a ramp, makes a swift U-turn, crosses the grassy median, and bolts down the road.

"You asked me a question. I went to get the answer," he says.

"Sorry, but I can't read your mind." *Or Baron's.*

"What made you get into the car without protection?"

"I didn't know." I shake my hands, whining like a teenager who's defending herself after breaking curfew.

"But I told you to stay still and wait."

"But you didn't!" I shake my hands again.

"I told you that you were not supposed to take the protection from the car."

All I can do is sigh. Apparently our communication styles are different. If there's a rule book on how we're supposed to work together and converse, I didn't get it, but I sure would like a copy. I decide to not argue with him any further because it's a lost cause. He has a different reality than I do.

"So what did Felix say? Will he see us?" I ask, changing the subject altogether.

"I am taking you to him." Viesel glances at

Lario through the rearview mirror then glares at the road.

I can't tell if he's angry, but I really don't want him to be upset. I know his intentions are to keep me safe, and I think he's not used to using words to communicate with anyone.

"Viesel Egos?" I cautiously say.

He peers at me through the mirror.

"We're going away from New York. Does that mean Felix is not there?" I ask.

It takes him a moment, but then he says, "No."

"Then where is he?"

Fawn shakes her head at me. "Clarity, don't push it."

I think Viesel Egos is going to leave it at that, allowing Fawn's words to speak for him. He takes his eyes off of me and puts them back on the road.

I wanted to go to New York and find a way to search for Baron. I want to know if Zina is truly his enemy or his lover. I turn to the one person in the car who would know the answers.

"Lario, can you tell me about Zina?" I ask. I catch his very quick glimpse at Fawn.

He asks, "What do you want to know?"

"Was Baron ever in love with her?"

This time, he definitely looks at Fawn for permission, and she nods.

"They were grouped," he says.

"What does that mean?" There's a bite in my tone. I think I'm mad. If not mad, then I'm mildly upset. The word *grouped* sounds serious.

"They kept each other alive. They cured their thirst together."

I cut to the chase. "Did they make love?"

"Clarity, just—" Fawn says.

"No, I want to know. Did they make love?"

"I don't think what two vampires do is make love," Lario answers.

"Okay, sex. Did they have sex?"

He appears to be debating on whether to reveal the answer to that or not.

"Tell me," I insist.

"What they engaged in was more animalistic than mere sex."

As soon as Lario says it, my heart sinks so deep, I think it no longer exists. I've never been this hurt in my entire life. I gaze out the window and watch the world pass by. I can go to Enu now. I can run away from him now. But I don't want to leave Fawn.

"I've known Ze Feldis for hundreds of years," Lario continues after a moment of silence.

I don't look at him because if I do, I know for sure I'll cry. That would be too embarrassing.

"I never thought he'd make it this far as a vampire," Lario says. "He didn't like the hunt, but Zina gets a sick thrill out of convincing humans to give up their blood. You've seen Ze Feldis, and you've seen Zina?"

I turn to face him. "Yes."

"Humans worship beauty. It wasn't hard to talk a girl, even a boy, into giving up blood to get close to him. But there was one condition. Zina would tell his prey they couldn't speak to him while he drank them. I would think they died happy." He spreads his lips into a sarcastic grin that I'm starting despise seeing. "Drank and sometimes more by Ze Feldis the Beautiful."

I snarl at Lario. Jeez, he's such a prick. But I also remember seeing the vampire suck the blood out of the girl in the tunnel. He treated her like a milkshake in a cardboard cup. "How long does it take for the thirst to return?"

"A week, maybe two at the most."

"Is that all one life is worth? Two weeks?"

"That's all, folks," he says, wearing that cavalier grin.

I frown. I want to keep this serious. "And the human doesn't become a vampire?"

"Not if they're not turned."

"How is that done?"

Viesel Egos narrows his eyes at Lario. Lario and I both notice.

"Please tell me," I implore him.

Lario says, "A person has to drink the blood of a vampire before dying to become a vampire."

"Like in folklore?"

"Yes, sure, like in folklore."

I stop to think. "But why would you do that? Why would you choose to be a vampire?"

"You'd be amazed what you'll do for self-preservation. It was only after I was turned that I learned about the thirst. That's when I realized I chose wrong." He looks at Fawn, who's been listening quietly. "Well, that's until I met Fawn."

I study them as they smile at each other. They do look truly in love. However, one thing Lario said keeps gnawing me.

"I will never choose to be a vampire," I say. "Never." I love my soul. I'd rather be natural than supernatural, but it occurs to me that I've never been human."

"Well," Lario says, "if I had to choose again, I wouldn't choose differently. My dust would be over three hundred years old, and I would've never met your super-sexy sister."

Fawn leans in for a passionate kiss. Then Lario remembers I'm in the car. He forces his eyes away from Fawn and back on me.

"You had the same effect on Ze Feldis. See"—Lario leans toward me—"he can never be free of Zina. She tricked him once and drank a swallow of his blood. Now she can always find him no matter where he goes."

"But not under protection?"

"She knows he's there, but she can't enter it."

I happen to glance at Viesel and see him studying me. I think he's marking my reactions. It's as if he's not seeing me but seeing through me.

Then it dawns on me. "That's why he has to kill her!"

That's if he still wants to kill her. Baron didn't fling her off of him when she slid onto his lap and licked his neck; it was one of the other vampires who did that. Baron didn't go after her. He took his blade to the six vampires who had no hold on him.

I know Fawn has read my thoughts, because she's staring at me. From the look on her face, she thinks my questions are valid.

At some point, I fall asleep again. In the middle of the night, the car stops, and I wake up. We're at a rest stop, and Viesel stands at the back of the car gassing up. Lario isn't in the car, but Fawn is sleeping next to me. I'm starving. I see a Burger King and a Dairy Queen here, but all I want are berries and cream and Goshem tea.

I lightly shake Fawn's knee. "Hey."

She opens her eyes and looks around.

"Restroom and food. Are you in?" I ask.

"Yep."

We get out of the car.

"Back in," Viesel orders, and we both freeze where we stand.

"We do get to pee, don't we?" I ask.

He actually looks as though he has to consider the answer to that. I close my eyes, take some of the protection off the car, and spread it over the entire establishment. Viesel must be able to see it because he looks up and over. I make a mental note of that.

"I'll put it back when we leave," I say. "By the way, do you want anything?"

"No," he replies.

I don't think he eats food. "Okay."

Fawn and I make our way inside, and the smell of fried meat and potatoes makes me want to dry heave. We have to eat something, so we stand there staring at the menu, hoping at least one item will appeal to us.

"I can do French fries," I say.

"It's just a fried potato. Shouldn't taste that bad," Fawn says.

We're not convinced. The girl behind the register is staring at us, mainly because she's wondering what's taking us so long. *It's the Burger King menu, for goodness' sake*, she's thinking.

"All right," I say as if I'm ordering a new car, "two small French fries."

She rings them up. "Anything to drink?"

I look at Fawn. She's been on our strange diet longer than I have. Her brows are crimped, and she's really trying to find an alternative to Goshem tea.

This is why I don't travel too far from home, she says to me.

I chuckle, and the girl behind the counter turns her mouth down.

"Two waters," Fawn orders.

The girl rolls her eyes and slams two tiny cups in

front of us. Before I can dig into my pocket for money, Lario puts a hundred-dollar bill on the counter.

The girl frowns. "Sorry, no bills larger than a twenty."

"You can keep the change, or make me hunt for a five-dollar bill and you can still keep the change." He winks at her.

The girl is coy about it, but she stuffs the hundred-dollar bill into the drawer. I read her mind out of curiosity. She's planning to take the change when she closes out.

He holds up the two tiny cups. "And they're going to need bigger cups than this."

She huffs as she rolls her eyes and sets two supersized cups in front of us.

Lario collects our fries and water as Fawn and I go use the restroom. I don't like public restrooms, so I keep my eyes closed the entire time, touching as little as possible. Fawn thinks it's funny and laughs at me from start to finish. When we leave that cramped, germ-infested toilet I really didn't have to use in the first place, I finally let go of the breath I've been holding.

"If you keep drinking Goshem tea and eating

the fruits and cream, you won't have to do that anymore," she says.

I tilt my head curiously. "Do you mean use the bathroom."

"Yes."

"But didn't you..."

"No. I didn't. I will after eating those French Fries though."

"Wow."

"We're not very human, Clarity."

WHEN WE RETURN TO THE CAR VIESEL EGOS IS already sitting behind the wheel, staring ahead.

"See," I say to him as I slide into the car, "that wasn't so bad."

"Seat belts," Viesel Egos barks.

I smile and click mine. The car drives off.

"I need it back," he says in a dry tone.

I remember I need to take the protection off the rest stop and put it back over the car. If I leave it behind, there it stays.

Viesel Egos is in a better mood after I return the protection, so I ask again. "So, Viesel Egos, where are we headed?"

He gives me that look again. It's akin to a parent who's threatening a child with a spanking.

"Miami, Florida," he answers, to my surprise.

Fawn and I smile at each other.

"Thanks, Egos," she says.

"Yes, thanks," I say.

I think his eyes smile as he glances at us in the rearview mirror. *Maybe not.*

FAWN AND I FORCE OURSELVES TO EAT THE GREASY sticks of potato, reminding ourselves that we have to eat something. With each bite, I dream of those purple and red berries that aren't quite blueberries and aren't quite raspberries. What is that cream? It's fresh and light, and if the Enuians don't eat meat, then it must not be made with milk.

"Fawn, what's in the cream? You know the cream that goes on the berries and bread?"

"It's made with pokki pods."

"Pokki pods?" I force another French fry in my mouth and chew.

"It's similar to a green bean except it's filled with sweet cream."

"Wow, that's incredible." I pretend that's exactly what I'm chewing on right now.

"I think it's Felix who makes sure I get a fresh delivery every month."

"Sounds like him," I say.

We stay awake the rest of the way and talk about trivial things, such as how Lario tried to set up a satellite dish on their roof when the technician refused to walk through the woods to get to their house. She tells me that Lario can stand to drink Goshem tea, but the berries and cream make him gag. She says he needs meat, and to prove it, he slides a big hamburger from the paper bag and takes a greedy bite. Fawn rolls her eyes.

They're shocked that I don't have many stories outside of school and work.

"No people?" Fawn asks.

"Well, there were people at my school and job."

"Did you have any friends? Every girl has a best friend or two in a lifetime. However else will you experience your first stab in the back?"

I just shrug. "I never had any friends."

"Okay, what about boyfriends?"

"Nope."

"Lies," Lario shouts. "You cannot be as exquisite as you are and never have at least one boyfriend."

I shake my head and shrug. "It's difficult to

make friends or boyfriends when you know what people are thinking and feeling before you even say hello."

We fall silent in the dark. We all close our eyes and get comfy.

"I get it," Fawn finally says.

I open my eyes and see Viesel Egos's glowing blue eyes again, studying me. After meeting his gaze, I turn to look out the window and wait for the sun to come up.

CHAPTER

TWENTY-SIX

I t's a gray, overcast day in Miami, Florida. I've visited the burgeoning metropolis on business before, and I always harbor mixed feelings about the place. I don't think I could ever get used to having palm trees with my skyscrapers or a tropical feel to my city. Those who live here apparently love it. The inhabitants never stop stomping the sidewalks or lounging on the outdoor patios of restaurants. In that way, it's a lot like Los Angeles, just without the stifling traffic and constant crowds. I swear LA has reached its population capacity.

I can tell it's a hot and muggy day by how sweat glistens on everyone's bare skin. They're wearing shorts, tank tops, and bikini tops, and lots of the guys have no shirts on at all. Sundresses seem to be in style for women, and I think they look like a comfortable way to brave the type of weather where everything sticks to your skin.

I assume we're going to stay in one of the tall buildings downtown, which is more of Felix's style, until we turn onto the Venetian Crossway and speed down a bridge over water. We enter a community with large homes, large gates, tall trees, tacky lawn ornaments, and ocean serving as most of the backyards.

Soon, Viesel Egos makes a sharp left turn and stops in front of one of those tall, black, wrought-iron gates.

Are you nervous? I ask Fawn.

I am, she replies.

I take a deep breath as the two parts of the gate automatically swing open. The car rolls up the trop-ical tree-lined drive and stops under a pergola. The car doors open, and we slide out the backseat. I look up at a four-story mansion made of lots of glass windows. It seemed fragile enough for a big, bad hurricane to huff and puff and blow it down.

Fawn must see the visual in my head of a wolf and this overstated mansion because she laughs at me. "You're very interesting, Clarity. Your tastes are very precise."

I think about that for a second. "I just like to feel safe."

"There's no *safe*, not anymore," Lario says.

He's the first to follow Viesel up the red clay brick steps to the frosted glass door. My first glance of the inside takes my breath away.

Sculptures are featured throughout the initial walk-in space that's too massive to be called a living room. These sculptures are all familiar because they're *mine*. How did he get them? I'd sold them all. I never wanted Felix to know I sculpted. I once mentioned that I was interested in art, and he gave me the stone face before moving on to the appropriate places to fulfill my intern requirements. So after a season of playing artist, I used to sell my work on eBay.

My dad is apparently the one who outbid everyone. I don't know how I feel about that. Maybe flattered, certainly shocked.

"Yours," Fawn says as she touches one of my favorites—a white limestone egg on the verge of hatching the world.

I had decided to play with mass and space in this one. It was sort of a kooky, sci-fi piece, yet I was proud of myself for pulling it off.

"Yeah," I say. I mean, it sort of proves he cares.

He could've just bought my pieces and shoved them all in a storage shed.

Molly appears in the circular archway that leads to another massive room. She's a thin, well put-together young woman who always wears pantsuits and keeps her deep brown hair in a tight ponytail. She looks to be in her early or mid-thirties, but she's so serious that one would think she's a lot older.

"Clarity, Fawn," she says. This is her usual greeting.

"Molly," we answer at the same time.

She turns her back on us, and we know we're supposed to follow. Fawn takes Lario's hand, and I walk right behind them. Viesel Egos is nowhere to be found. I almost wonder where he went. It would've been nice to see the dynamics between him and Felix.

We're led to a huge dining room, and the table is set with all sorts of exotic berries and fruits. My mouth waters at the sight of the cream, breads, and hot Goshem tea.

Molly walks past the spread and stops on the left side of the table. "Felix thought you might be hungry. After lunch, I'll show you to your rooms."

"Is Felix here?" I ask.

"Yes, he is."

"So is he joining us?"

"No."

"Okay…" Talking to her is like having a conversation with Viesel Egos. "So when will he grace us with his presence?"

"Soon."

"Okay then," I say, giving up.

Fawn and I glance at each other. I sit on one side of the table, she sits on the other side, and Lario sits down next to her. Fawn and I hoped for this type of feast upon arrival. Molly turns her back on us, and her tiny heels tap against the glossy marble floor as she walks off.

"Great," Lario says, searching up and down the table. "Nothing good here for me. Your father's making it very clear who's not welcome."

"You're always welcome, love." Fawn takes Lario by the chin, guides his mouth to hers, and kisses him tenderly.

I don't know why, but I'm grinning at them. I feel as if, in a strange way, we're all in love together. They share a romantic love, but we all share a familial love. I'm sure that's why Felix doesn't bar Lario from this house. Fawn loves him, and I love that she loves him.

Clarity? Fawn asks as she spreads the cream on bread.

I look at her.

Is he really here?

This time, I keep my eyes open and search for Felix's energy. I feel him near, but I can't pinpoint where he is. There's a stronger protection over this place. It extends far and wide, and I would really have to strain to take from it.

He's around. I glance over my shoulder. *He's somewhere to the rear of me.*

Do you still think we can get him to tell us where the gravesite is? she asks.

I look into her eyes. They're unsure and desperate—like everything is riding on getting that information.

I'll definitely try. I bite into my bread, cream, and berries, and a blast of flavors fill my mouth.

After we eat, Molly returns to show us to our rooms. She takes Fawn and Lario first, leaving me sitting at the table. I stare out the window at the dark ocean in the distance.

I can't help but think about the last time I saw Baron. Maybe he's gone from me forever. It could be for my own good. Who knows? I imagine that being with me, a person who is part divine, two parts Enuian, and a quarter human, put him a little over his head—well, a lot over his head. Although I know of my true family now, I also know that the time has to come when I'll make my way in this world for myself.

Before Molly returns, I walk back to that space that holds my sculptures. Does he think I'm talented? I smooth a hand over the rock sculpture of a butterfly I carved. It's black and white, and I used the pattern of the rock to play with color. That's when it hits me. It's the insect called a Wek. I shaved tiny dents in the wings and the top of the head to represent polka dots.

"Clarity."

I jump and turn to see Molly.

"Felix will see you now."

"But what about—"

"He will speak only to you," she says.

I stop myself from tuning into Fawn as I follow Molly. We go in the opposite direction of where she took Fawn and Lario, through what looks like an observation room made of nothing but glass. The city of Miami is in view on one side, the ocean on the other side, and the cloudy gray sky above. Once we get through there, we go down a set of white parquet stairs. Down and down we go, deeper than what I ascertained is the length of this four-story home. Just when I'm about to ask if we're there yet, I see the end and what appears to be an entrance to a well-lit room.

Molly stops at the door. "In there." She steps back to let me pass.

I hesitate, collect my confidence, and walk through. A blast of light engulfs me. I can see nothing ahead of or behind me, but I keep moving. I end up on a deck, facing a cloudless day with a topaz sky and clear white waters as far as my eyes can see.

Then I see him. Felix stands against the crystal rail with his back turned to me.

"Felix," I barely call.

When he turns around, he has the same effect on me as usual. If I had to choose one word to define my father, it would be *regal*. His skin is the color of fine brass, and all his features are sharp—cheekbones, mouth, and chin. His forehead is smooth. He could play the pharaoh in a *Cleopatra* remake.

"Hi," I say. I half expect him to plan the rest of my life from this moment forward.

"You've met your sister," he says.

"Yes, I have."

"Good." He walks over to a set of lounge chairs I didn't see at first. "Come join me."

My feet are heavy, but I walk over and sit beside him.

At first, he doesn't say anything but continues to stare ahead. "And she's brought company," he finally says. I can't tell if he thinks that's good or bad.

"Lario."

"The one who ate the leaf."

I nod.

"And now he's here with my daughters."

"But he's human," I say in Lario's defense.

"He's not human." My dad looks at me with those penetrating hazel eyes. "He ate a leaf of the Tree of Life."

I gulp. This conversation is not going the way I pictured it.

"Do you know what that means?" he asks.

I shake my head like the coward I am.

"This Lario can be stabbed a million times and not die until his appointed time, which is three hundred and thirty-nine years. He's already used up three hundred and thirty-seven of them."

This new information whacks me in the head so hard that for a second, I lose focus. My mind does the easy math until… "That means he only has two years to live." I sound as though the breath has been knocked out of me.

"You've been to their dwelling, haven't you?"

"Yes." My heart is thumping.

"You've seen the books? He's smart."

"For the most part."

"Do you think he knows this about himself? That his ambitions put the nail in his coffin?"

I frown, wondering where Felix is going with this. "You don't trust him?"

Felix stares into my eyes until one side of his mouth lifts in a snarl. "I don't."

I'm taken aback. I've never seen my father this angry about anything. He's an even kind of guy, stoic.

"You have the power of the mind. The strongest of the seven," he says. "He knows how to keep you out only because of how little you know about yourself, and I take the blame for that. I want you to know you can stop armies in their tracks. You can hear the whispers of an ant if you desire. You can *certainly* penetrate any shield Lario Exgesis forms."

I think the last part of that got away from Felix. I see him take a deep breath to steady himself.

"Do you know what else you can do?" he asks after calming himself.

I shake my head. "No."

"Search his heart, find that leaf, and rip it out of him."

"But will he be a vampire again?"

"He will, but that's what he's supposed to be."

I remember the thirst. How is that supposed to be anyone's lot? "I can't do it. I felt the thirst, and I know he'd rather be dead than feel like that forever."

Felix lets out a cynical grunt. "That's you, Cl'auta. You're not Exgesis."

"I still can't."

"But I can," Felix growls. "And I will."

"Why are you telling me this? Why don't you just do it?" Simply put, I'm angry because I feel as if I'm being manipulated. My head spins as I watch a creature in the middle of the crystal ocean flip up out of the water and fall back in. I let that amazing sight sooth me as I wait for Felix's answer. When I don't get one, my mouth tells him what I'm thinking. "I think you already know that this will destroy her."

"She'll get over it as long as she has—someone."

I sniff sarcastically. "Is that someone me? Because I'm not Lario. I can't give her what he gives her."

Again, he's silent. I know he's thinking. My father and I are similar in that way.

"Maybe. Maybe not," he finally says, looking far off.

"I don't agree with you about him. I'm positive he loves her. If he hasn't told her how long he has to live, then I'm sure he has a pretty good reason."

"I doubt his reason is good," Felix spits.

"How do you know? Have you read his mind?"

Felix goes silent, which answers the question for me.

"You can't read his mind?" I ask.

"Because she gave him the leaf and he ate it, he holds Fawn's human soul within him. He can hear everything I say to her unless you or I take the leaf out of him."

"Is that why I can't hear him?"

"I told you—Exgesis has found a way to block you out of his mind," Felix says. "But all you have to do is mentally break that boundary. However, you've also sworn yourself to protect Fawn, and because of that, he can manipulate you in ways

Fawn never would. You shouldn't swear yourself to protect your sister, Cl'auta."

Now I'm doing the silent thinking. How did I swear myself to protect her? How can I undo it?

"Swear yourself to a larger cause," he answers. "The one you came here to speak to me about."

"Discovering our purpose?"

"You've remembered the map?"

His going right to the source of our meeting tells me I answered correctly. "I have."

"Give me your hand."

I open my palm, and Felix takes my hand. I feel and see a flash of light rush through me until I squeeze my eyes tight. Only when the map becomes as visible as it was on the page do I relax my face.

Felix still clutches my hand. "Open your eyes, Cl'auta. Never close them. You don't need to. But hold the map in your mind."

I open my eyes but still think about the map. It's difficult at first—like the first time I held Adore out of my mind or when I pushed peace over a rabid mob of drivers.

"Relax," he says. "You're able to do this as easily as slicing air with a blade."

I take a deep breath, and when I let it out, I relax the tension in my shoulders and neck.

"That's better." His voice sounds soothing. "Now, I'm going to give you this."

A ball of light bounces on top of the ocean. It races toward me, and I brace myself for the impact. When it hits me, there's an explosion of light in my head, and I feel warm all over.

"Now you and only you know the way," he says. "It won't be easy getting there. But if you think it, be it, and stay within yourself, then you should be fine." He lets go of my hand with another flash of light. "This is where I'll be when you return. No matter what, bring the book to me. Only to me, Cl'auta."

We sit in silence. A circle of creatures are flipping in and out of the water. I see them more clearly now. They look like dolphins, but they're not. Their skin is a purplish color, and their bodies are thin and long.

"What are those?" I ask Felix.

"Sickels."

"Sliders?"

"Yes."

We enjoy the show in silence for a short while.

TWENTY-SEVEN

When I walk out of Felix's secret portal to Enu, I think I'm about to rush up the winding stairs to his Miami home, but I don't. I come out of the portal onto a deserted beach. The black water, darkened sky, and pieces of trash tell me I'm back on Earth.

It isn't nighttime yet, but the sun has dropped. I look at a long wooden dock to my left, and standing there in the purpling evening, wearing black slacks and a long black coat, is Viesel Egos. I know he's there to collect me, so I trod through the mushy, damp sand toward him.

When I get to the edge of the dock, Viesel Egos gives me his outstretched hand. I see wooden stairs to the far right, but since he's offering, I take his hand. I feel as light as a leaf when he pulls me up, and I land solidly on my feet.

"Thanks," I say with a smile.

His brow furrows. He nods once and starts toward the end of the dock where a speedboat is waiting. As our boat speeds through the water, I waste no time doing what Felix tells me to do. I think about the seven sisters and our grandmother, Zillael. Then it hits me—Felix didn't warn me about Baron Ze Feldis. I wonder why.

I had considered giving Baron a leaf from the Tree of Life to take away his thirst so that we could live together, sort of like Fawn and Lario. Now I know that's a faulty solution. If the leaf doesn't kill him on the spot, then it will eventually.

Until now, all I wanted to do was save Baron; maybe that's selfish of me. Maybe my goals should reach further than that. If there's a greater good, then maybe that was why Fawn couldn't send those innocent people flying to their deaths on the freeway. I too must see past my love for Baron Ze Feldis and my new sister's happiness and security, and I must act in favor of a greater cause, whatever that may be.

The four-tiered glass house glows in the

distance. Never have I felt so alone. The information Felix laid upon me is heavy indeed. I'm almost reluctant to connect with Fawn now. If what Felix told me is true and Fawn and Lario are linked, then he must have heard me speak in her head all along.

This time, I make sure I single in on her and only her. *Fawn, are you there?*

Where have you been for the last two days? she asks.

"It's her," she says to Lario, who's near her.

I dig hard to separate Lario from Fawn until I know I feel and hear them both separately. *I've been in Enu with Felix*, I say only to Fawn.

Lario is wondering why he can't hear me, but he hasn't mentioned it to Fawn. So he *can* hear everything I've said to her up until now, and she knows nothing about it. My heart is heavy, but I let him back in so as not to tip him off.

It's been two days. We were worried about you, she says. *I looked all over this monster-sized house for you.*

Sorry—but he gave me what we needed.

Where are you now? She still sounds frantic.

On my way in.

The boat pulls up to the dock, and I get out of it before Viesel Egos can reach over to help me. I run up the plank, heading for the steps, but before I can reach the house's back door, something pulls me off my path. The next thing I know, familiar, warm lips are pressed against mine. A warm tongue carefully tastes my mouth, and I do some savory tasting myself. Emotions flood me as my head feels as if it's floating.

Open your eyes, I tell myself. The face I've been longing to see is here.

"I missed you," Baron whispers between kisses.

"I missed you too," I say.

"I need you, Clarity."

My legs are wrapped around his waist until I remember what I had been doing before he caught me. I force myself out of his grasp. "I have to see Fawn. Can you come in?"

"Yes." He cups an arm around my waist and swoops me into the house.

Fawn and Lario are in the room with the sculptures. When she sees me, she runs over and hugs me tightly.

"I had no idea what happened to you. You scared me," she says, shaking like a leaf.

"I'm sorry," I say. "I swear, I was only there for fifteen minutes. But I must have lost time here. Where's Molly? She didn't tell you?"

"She's gone, although she didn't say anything to us."

"That's strange," I say. "But we should talk." I look at Lario specifically. "All of us."

"Follow me," Fawn says. "I know this place like the back of my hand now. I've been through it about a hundred times."

"Isn't that a tad bit exaggerated?" Lario says.

That was meant to be a cute little joke, but Fawn isn't laughing. She frowns as she moves down the hallway, opening doors with her mind instead of her hands. She's upset because Felix left her out of the rendezvous in Enu.

Fawn? I ask, again freezing out Lario.

"Here," she says as we enter a lounge full of plush sofas and chairs. *Clarity?* she answers.

I'm relieved she replied. For a second, I thought she was angry enough at me to ignore me. We all take a seat. Baron sits next to me, and his nearness is extremely distracting. I have this overwhelming desire to indulge in the energy that being close to him stirs up. Plus, I have a few questions to ask him as well.

Did you know Lario can hear everything in your head?

"What?" she shouts and scowls at Lario.

Please let me explain before you lay into him, I urge.

"What?" he asks her with wide eyes, totally confused.

She narrows her eyes at him. "Nothing." She focuses on me but gives him the cold shoulder.

I look at Baron. "Will you be able to listen to this if you and Zina are still linked?"

"Who told you we were linked?" Baron asks.

Lario lifts a finger. Baron glares at him with a low growl rumbling in his throat.

"I had to," Lario says. "Believe me, you'd be deep in the doghouse if I didn't. True?" He looks at me for confirmation.

I take a moment to consider *all* that he told me about Baron and Zina—about how she's enthralled by him and how her infatuation drove her to keep him alive. "True. Now tell her." I stare at Lario.

"Tell who what?" Lario is wide-eyed and confused. He's a little suspicious but superior enough to think he hasn't been figured out by us meek women.

"Tell Fawn that you can hear it when I speak to her in her head."

"Is it true?" Fawn asks.

He's speechless.

"Is it true?" she insists.

He's anxious but fighting it. He's actually debating about whether to come clean or not. He glimpses at me, aware that I can hear him now. "It's true."

"Why have you kept this from her?" I ask.

"I don't want to hurt your sister. I love her."

I eye him suspiciously. His love for Fawn is the only emotion he has right now. It almost feels fabricated. I turn to Fawn. Her eyes are watery, and her heart is on the verge of being broken.

"I think we should all go to our rooms for the rest of the night, and we'll talk tomorrow," I suggest.

Fawn stands and heads out. Lario gives me the *why* look before following her. I sit still, hoping I haven't ruined what looked to be a pretty solid love story.

"Are you okay?" Baron asks.

What's strange is that I almost forgot he was sitting there. "I had to tell her the truth, right?"

"Absolutely," Baron says. "Exgesis has been known to get in over his head. He can be harmless, but he doesn't think hard enough about his actions. The will of the wind can send him into a superficial tailspin, which at times can be harmful."

"Are you saying he's dangerous?"

"I'm saying I'm always cautious when I get involved with Exgesis. He seems to have always loved your sister, but I'd advise you to be cautious for her."

"Wow," I say. "I thought you two were friends."

"Vampires don't have friends."

"But he's human."

"Not in his heart—or maybe in his heart. Who says a human's heart is pure? Mine wasn't."

I'm taken aback again. He's corroborating all of Felix's warnings. "I'll be cautious. For her."

"Of course you will," he says, smirking.

There's a shift in his mood. The vampire is back and gazing into my eyes. A part of me wants him to tear my clothes off right here and now and gratify me like only he can. The other part wants him to answer for his relationship with Zina until I'm no longer feeling insecure. The last part wants him to hold me, pull me into him, and never, ever let me go.

"I guess I should find a room," I say with a sigh.

In a swift movement I hardly feel, Baron picks me up. We move through the halls and up the stairs, until we're in a bedroom. I fall onto the bed. My tank top is off, my pants are off, and I'm in nothing but my underwear, a sight he seems to relish.

I feel something deeper for him tonight. "Wait." I lift my arms to him. "Please hold me."

Without a moment's pause, he's cradling me tight. I'm under the sheet, but he isn't.

We stay like this for a long while. I stare out into the ocean beyond the glass walls. I want to check in on Fawn and Lario, but I don't want to intrude even more. I want to ask Baron if he made love—or had steamy sex—with the vampire he's linked to while he was away, but I'm not ready to hear the answer to that. I'm sure he feels the unease gripping me.

He asks, "What did Exgesis tell you about Zina?" He says her name with a bite.

I sigh with relief, glad he's getting the conversation started. "That she used to bring humans to you to quench your thirst. That she drank your blood, which is why you're linked."

"He told you that, huh?"

I nod. "Yes. Is it true?"

"Most of it. That's not why she's linked to me though. All vampires are linked. That's the true danger of us."

"So does that mean you belong to her and she belongs to you? She can follow you here, can't she?"

"No, I belong to you, Clarity. You belong to me." He flips me around to face him. "I want you to always remember that. You don't have to worry about Zina. I'm going to end her."

"I can help you do that, you know—end her." I sound unsure of myself.

"You're not a killer. And you're already helping me."

"But what if she kills you first?"

"She's crazed, but Zina doesn't want me dead. She wants you dead, but I'll kill her before that happens."

There's an earnest look in his eye, which makes me kiss the tip of his nose. Every kiss with him is so warm, it's unreal. Then I remember I have another question for him.

"Why did you have to kill the six vampires? You know, when I saw you in the tunnels?"

He's silent for a moment. "You saw that?"

"I did."

"I'm sorry you had to see that."

"Don't be," I say between kisses.

Our kissing gets hot and heavy. In one rapid movement, Baron pulls back, slips his black T-shirt off, and takes off his black slacks. We're both almost nude. The ripples of his muscles take my breath away. I imagine him as a marble block before me, and I see myself carving him into real life. Although he is not my creation, he belongs to me.

If I'm the sculptor, then he's the painter. I feel

all ten of his fingers caress my calves. Something different is stirring within me. Heat starts at the tips of my toes and rushes through me, like ocean waves under the influence of the full moon.

"What's happening?" I ask breathlessly and lift my head to look down at my feet.

My eyes expand. What I'm seeing is not possible —my skin is glowing. I'm alarmed, and I gaze at Baron. His hands have not stopped smoothing my thighs. It appears as if our skin touching generates this light.

His touch makes me feel as if I'm being wrapped in a soft blanket fresh out of the dryer or bathing in the late-afternoon sun on a perfect day. When he presses himself gently on top of me, that's how my entire body feels. I'm soaring through light and heat. I'm inside Baron Ze Feldis, and he's inside me. His lips slide down to my mouth. He's groaning in delight, and so am I.

Baron's supple tongue slips down the front of my neck. He unhooks my bra's front clasp and peels the material away from breasts. I whimper as he sucks my nipple into his deliciously warm mouth.

My body is exploding with pleasure, need, desire. He licks and kisses down my belly as he slowly pulls my panties down my legs. Then his hot mouth latches on to my pleasure spot.

I cry out and sink my fingers into the bed sheets. The tickling sensation explodes in my groin. It's almost too much to bear. I think I'm trying to squirm and get away from him, but he holds me steady. I've lost my head.

Here it comes…

It's coming…

I scream.

He inserts himself inside me, and the tickling sensation rebuilds. We kiss feverishly, grabbing at each other and smoothing each other. Our hands, bodies, and mouths can't get enough of each other. Then he pitches his head back and unleashes a series of growls as my orgasm almost makes me white out.

I can't mark the time when it ended. All I know is that he's cradling me, and sparks of light are still flickering in our bodies. We lie with our limbs entangled on top of the bed.

"What was that? You know, the light," I whisper.

After a long moment, he says, "I wish I knew, but it felt damn good."

"Yeah," I whisper. "I indubitably agree." I look

up at him, grinning. He presses his lips against mine, and we make out.

"How do you feel?" He has a concerned look on his face.

"Exhausted," I say.

"I thought so."

"How do you feel?" I ask in return.

"I feel like I love you."

I sniff a chuckle. Not at his declaration of love, which doesn't go unnoticed, but because there's no part of me that doesn't know he loves me. I flip over to face him. "Are you thirsty?"

"No, but I haven't been thirsty since the last time we were together."

"Really?" This is news to me.

"Really."

I kiss him again, and the light flickering through our bodies moves to our mouths. Everywhere we touch, it goes there also. I pull back. It's getting eerie.

"I think I want to be asleep for three days straight." I flip around to face away from him.

He wraps his arms around me. "Clarity, I—"

"I know." His tone tells me what he was going to say. "I'll be taking a trip as well," I whisper.

The move is too quick, but I'm on my back, and he's on top of me.

"To where?" he demands.

I stare deep into his eyes. "If I tell you, will she be able to know? You guys are bonded, sort of."

"Everybody's not like you, Clarity. She can't read my mind."

I ponder that. It's hard for me to accept that I'm special. Everyone has either thought it or treated me as if I'm special, and all I ever wanted was to be normal. Because of that, I normalized myself.

"I'm going to find a book about me and my sisters," I say.

"Sisters? There are more of you?"

I hesitate, wondering if I should divulge this information to a vampire. He flips me again until I'm on top of him, and his tender lips tastes mine. I feel more than loved by him; I feel relished.

I tell him how Felix came to be and about our mother, Crystalline. Then I tell him about the seven of us and about Zillael, our grandmother.

"But your father said it's going to be dangerous?"

"*Can* be dangerous. He also said I'm equipped to deal with it."

He shakes his head. "I'll go with you."

After he says that, I'm lying beside him on my back. I'm getting used to being gently moved around by him. "But what about Zina?"

He gets up and flips a switch on the wall near the door. Shades slide down over all the glass.

"I'll handle *her*. Let's make love," he says.

He's back inside me, thrusting. I hold him tightly. Already, I'm starting to climax.

CHAPTER

TWENTY-EIGHT

"Are you telling me Ze Feldis is onboard?" Lario yells from the kitchen where he's frying eggs in one pan and bacon in the other.

"That's what he said," I shout, making sure I sound cheerful enough.

Fawn and I sit at the table eating berries, cream, and bread. She hasn't looked away from her plate or spoken since we took our chairs. She's not in the best mood, and it's all because of me.

I'm sorry for telling you what I told you yesterday, I say to her only.

After a moment, she looks at me and smiles. *You haven't wronged me, Cl'auta. Lario has.*

I chew on my bottom lip. *Did you talk last night?*

We did.

Did he tell you why he kept the secret?

Because he wanted me to believe the leaf had the effect we thought it would. We made our plans around him being a hundred percent human.

I have something else to tell you. I brace myself. *He only has two years to live.*

She goes rigid. I can tell by how she's looking at me that this is news to her.

Does Lario know? I ask.

I'd be shocked if he does. He would tell me. Wouldn't he? she asks me with wide, childlike eyes.

Lario trots into the dining room carrying his plate. He slides into the seat beside Fawn. "Now this is real food." He winks at Fawn and stabs a load of fried eggs with his fork.

She smiles weakly. He's trying too hard to make the moment light. It's clear things have changed between them.

"Lario…" Her voice is quieter than I ever heard it. "Do you know how long you have to live?"

I watch his every body movement and use my ability to gather his thoughts and feel his emotions. He knows, but he knows something else. *Fawn is going to die in two years with him.* I control my reaction to this revelation and choose to keep it to myself.

"Yes, I did know," he confesses.

"But why——" Fawn says.

"Because I don't need you worrying about me. We're going to fix this, okay?"

She touches his face, and he takes her hand and kisses it. I look away from them. The organ in my chest called a heart feels like a lump of steel. I can't stop my eyes from watering, but I call upon the years where I had to be strong in order to stop the tears from falling.

Four days ago, I believed Fawn and Lario's love was so uncomplicated, but after learning he's still keeping one very big secret from Fawn, all of my hopes for them have turned to ashes.

I SPEND THE REST OF THE DAY MAKING OUR TRAVEL plans. I place a call to Felix's charter service and schedule a flight for four into Cairo, leaving at nine forty-five p.m. As the instructions within me specify, I make arrangements for the airplane to taxi into a private hangar upon arrival, one with no windows, where Baron will stay until sundown. What's strange is Felix already knew Baron would be joining us.

While Baron sleeps and Fawn and Lario take

more time to talk, I ask Viesel to take me shopping for clothes that are suitable for the desert. Other than the dress and shoes I bought in the airport, I've never shopped for my own clothes. This is pathetic, I know. When Viesel Egos asks where I'd like to go, the first place that comes to mind is Saks Fifth Avenue. Freda really likes shopping there.

He nods once. I follow him to the car, the right back door opens on its own, and I slide in. Viesel Egos drives over the bridge, takes a series of turns in the city, and we end up at Saks. I search high and low for something appropriate; the clothes are very high-end. After hours of searching, I find a few pairs of fashionable yet comfortable cargo pants, a black and dark brown soft cotton T-shirt, and lace-up boots that aren't quite hiking boots, but they'll do.

AT NINE FORTY-FIVE P.M., BARON, FAWN, LARIO, and I enter the charter plane. To all of our surprise, Viesel Egos joins us.

In a swift move, Baron is only inches away from Viesel Egos' face. "She doesn't need you here. I'll protect her."

"In the daylight, *vampire*?" Viesel Egos growls.

They face off in silence for a few more moments, and then Baron stands beside me. Viesel Egos makes a sharp turn into the cockpit and closes the door. That's the end of the brief showdown.

"Ze Feldis, did you just snap off at our pilot?" Lario jokes.

Baron pulls his mouth tight. He doesn't like that Viesel Egos is with us. Baron sits beside me and goes stiff. He doesn't even look at me after we strap in, take off, and level at the right altitude. I sneak peeks at him for a while, wondering what I did to make him brood in this manner.

"Are you mad at me?" I whisper. I glance up and over the top of the seat in front of me. Fawn and Lario have pulled their seats into beds and are spooning.

"Why would I be mad at you, Clarity?" he asks, but his tone does not put me at ease.

"I don't know. You tell me."

He doesn't say a word. He only closes his eyes and freezes me out even more. I hate this. Our shoulders touch, and the warmth makes me want more. I think about what he could be so upset about.

"Are you upset because I asked Viesel Egos to take me shopping today?"

He remains quiet and tense.

I lean into him. "Look, he drives the car, and I needed a ride. Plus, he kept me safe. Don't you like that?"

"I'm the one who should keep you safe," he says calmly, his eyes still closed.

"You're jealous?"

"I'm not jealous; I just don't like the guy."

I shake my head. This reaction to Viesel Egos taking me to buy clothes makes no sense. He knows Viesel has to drive me where I need to go. Viesel Egos has grown on me, and I trust him. Baron doesn't have to be Einstein to figure that out.

I glance at Lario. I wonder what he said to Baron. I try to get into his head, but I hear nothing but air. Right now, he's feeling nothing but love for Fawn. I'm certain this is his defense against my ability. I glance at Fawn, and she looks so safe and comfortable in his arms. I don't know what to think about Lario any longer, other than what's ingrained in me—*hold on to the hope.*

"Get up," I whisper in Baron's ear.

In a moment, he's out of his seat and standing in the aisle, looking down at me. I don't think I'll ever get used to his super speed. After gathering my bearings, I stand. Just as I start to transform our seats into a bed, he takes over and finishes the task for me.

"Thought we should lie down," I say.

Once again, he moves swiftly. We're lying face to face beside each other.

"I don't want to hate that he gets to be with you when I can't. I'll try to control my anger. I promise," he whispers.

I stare into his eyes and kiss his lips. "You're the only vampire for me."

And there goes my favorite expression of his— he smirks back at me. "Viesel Egos is not a vampire."

I reach up to smooth his brow. "Listen, I love *you*. I think this is a forever thing we've got going on between us. Don't you?"

"Of course I'll love you forever, Clarity." He sounds offended that I would think otherwise.

"So you don't have to be jealous of Viesel Egos. We need him." I whisper very lightly, "If you knew everything, you'd understand."

"What do you mean?"

I touch his forehead. "Can I?"

He seems confused, but I push into his mind anyway. I'm inside him, and within Baron Ze Feldis is not a deep dark place. It's hollow. It's foggy. But I feel safe.

Fawn can die in two years along with Lario because she gave him the leaf from the Tree of Life, I say to him before taking my hand off his forehead. We stare at each other. I'm glad he understands the magnitude of the burden I've been carrying.

We press our lips together, and I close my eyes to think. In a matter of hours, I will be on the ground. The way to the gravesite is in me; getting there will be instinctual. According to Felix, we will meet aggression. In my head, I see the gigantic trees bending like straw, pushed by the power of *the evil*. It was relentless in its chase, even if it couldn't subdue me because of the protection. Realizing I'm frightening myself, I let Baron pull me into him.

"Making love to you was magnificent," he whispers.

I smile. "Ditto."

He bumps his burgeoning hard-on against me. "Too bad we're not alone."

I twist around to kiss him. "Too bad."

Although we can't keep our hands off of each other, at some point, I fall asleep.

CHAPTER

TWENTY-NINE

It's hot in Cairo—one hundred twenty degrees in the shade provided by the ledge of the hangar's roof. Baron remains on the airplane in the hangar as planned. We're not waiting long before a military-style black Humvee darts down the concrete drive and comes to a grinding halt in front of us. The driver, a short, stocky guy in a long, powder blue *kurta* shirt and pant set, steps out of the driver's seat.

"Let's move out," Viesel Egos says.

Fawn and Lario climb into the backseat. I'm on my way to the passenger-side seat when Viesel Egos touches my shoulder. I stop in my tracks.

"Give me your hand," he tells me.

I take his outstretched hand. I expect an explosion or something because of him being the creature he is and me being what I am. After a long moment, he lets go of my hand. I experienced nothing.

I'm a connoisseur of cities, and Cairo, Egypt, is a bustling metropolis. It's a sand-colored explosion of buildings that mirrors modern Roman architecture with its bulky cement structures and tall windows and balconies. Out of nowhere, an ultra-phallic, grandiose building—erected to convince the world that they're contemporary-minded—pops up. The mosques have the more circular and domed Islamic accents, but the European design influence is abundant in the main city.

It's late afternoon, and lots of men walk around in lightweight *kurta* sets. Some men are in more Western attire—slacks and button-down plaid shirts. A few women are sprinkled throughout in their *abayas* and *jilbabs*, but they move like ghosts in the forest.

We're stopped at a crosswalk when a small group of men pause their conversation to glare at me.

"Stop pulling from them," Viesel Egos scolds me.

That's when I realize the reason I've been

focusing on the masculine parts of the city is because that's the dominant energy. I've been pulling on it because I'm anxious about the unknown aggression we'll soon be facing. Once I follow Viesel Egos's instructions, the men return to their conversation.

"Thanks," I mutter.

"Fear is good. Stay prepared and stay in control, both of you." He glances at Fawn through his rearview mirror.

I glance over my shoulder at her, and she smiles at me. We take each other's hand for a moment. We haven't discussed what's to come. We've been warned enough to know it won't be a cakewalk, but what sort of plan can we make when we have no idea what we're going to encounter?

Viesel Egos runs through the rest of the stoplights just like he did during my first car ride with him. He's not causing a disturbance, and no one notices the tons of steel bolting down the street. To my surprise, we pull into the drive of the grandiose Grand Hyatt hotel.

"This is where the human stays," Viesel says after Lario's door opens.

"No way," Lario says, refusing to exit the Humvee.

"Get out, or I will remove you myself," Viesel says without a hint of fury. It's clear he means to do as he claims.

"But he has to be with me. I won't go without him," Fawn cries and scoots out of the vehicle too.

Viesel doesn't move to stop her. I look at him, but he's really going to let them both go. I grab Fawn's arm before she's all the way out.

"Wait," I plead. "Viesel Egos, why does Lario have to stay here?"

Viesel Egos just glares at me as if he doesn't owe us an explanation.

"Come on, please just tell her something. I need her with me. Aren't two sisters better than one?" I say.

"When we're out of the city, we'll travel by air," Viesel offers.

"By airplane?"

"No, by the air."

After hearing that, Lario puts his hand on Fawn's shoulder to stop her from following him. "He's right. I can't travel by air. I'm human." His top lip curls a little.

I sense he despises that fact.

"But—" Fawn starts.

"As a vampire, I could, but as a man, I can't.

Go. Clarity is stronger with you than without you. I'll see you all as soon as you get back with the book." He stares at me for reassurance.

I glare into his eyes, giving him none. Fawn looks over her shoulder at me and then back at Lario. She's torn.

"Go," Lario says again.

Fawn and Lario kiss more passionately than I've ever seen them kiss. He forces himself to pull away first and helps her scoot back into the vehicle. He turns his back as if it'll kill him to see her go off without him, and he trots into the hotel lobby. I notice how Viesel Egos narrows his eyes at Lario. He doesn't like Baron, but he *really* doesn't like Lario. I wish Viesel Egos were the explaining, conversing, instructing type, but alas, he's not. I'll probably never know why he hates Lario so much.

"Fawn—" I start.

"Just go," she orders Viesel, who wastes no time putting us on the road.

It's hard to imagine that we can physically move faster than a speeding car. Once we end our silent ride into Helwan, Viesel Egos turns into a shanty made of thin, rippled tin. Inside, men in greasy *kurtas* eye Fawn and me as we get out of the car. I gather their initial reaction to us, and it's not good.

If Viesel Egos were not with us and we were normal human women, we'd be in a pickle. If Viesel Egos *weren't* with us and we were the creatures that we are, then they'd be in trouble.

"Can I take the protection with us?" I ask Viesel.

"No," he snaps. "It stays here."

Fawn and I stare at each other with wide, nervous eyes.

"So we're going out there unprotected?" she asks.

"You have what's in you." Viesel strides out of the garage and into the bright day.

Fawn and I stare at each other.

Are you ready? she asks.

As I'll ever be.

I look around at the men side-eyeing us. I dig within myself and push out *indifference*, and suddenly they look away from us. The two who are eating lunch go back to reading their newspapers, and the other three go back to working on a late-model German car.

Fawn knows I created the mood. She nods at me, and I nod back. Outside, Viesel stands along the side of the dusty two-lane highway. He's a ghostly-looking figure in all black. Any regular person would be burning up in those thick, dark clothes, but he doesn't break a sweat. He watches us approach, and when we reach him, he turns to face the road.

"Keep up," he says.

Before we know it, he's a blur in black, heading upward and south. I don't even think about it; I strive to follow after him, and I'm doing it *somehow*. This is what it means to ride the wind. Although the air is stifling and the heat cooks the inside of my throat, I'm walking on air!

I've had dreams of doing this, of soaring high above the ground. But what's even stranger is that I'm actually walking. My legs are moving left, right, left, right. Rather than moving at record speed, it's as though we're taking giant steps. *This is unbelievable.*

Fawn and I catch up with Viesel Egos, and together, all three of us move above the Nile River. I'm awed by the pyramids and sphinxes below. I can't imagine having all that material to sculpt with. I always thought there were only two sphinxes, but there are hundreds of them. The merging of the old and new is nothing short of amazing.

The sight below makes me lose focus until we hit the edge of thick fog. Viesel stops, and we follow suit. The vapors surround us. Visibility is low, and the air turns cooler by the second.

"Clarity, how close are they?" Viesel Egos is alert and has one hand inside his coat.

I widen my eyes, confused, because that comes off like a trick question. He's speaking to me as if I know what I'm supposed to do, and I'm too afraid to ask because whoever or whatever is out there might be close. My instincts take over. I think the word *clear* and charge forward through the fog.

The fog extends past Luxor and into the dry, stony deserts of Sudan. That's where I feel them. There are three of them moving in our direction very quickly. They're looking around because they sense me. I know what the white figures treading the soft sands of the Nubian Desert are—they're vampires. One of them sees me and hits one of the others on the chest. He points up, and now all three of them are squinting at me.

I snap back to myself. "They're coming."

I must admit, I'm afraid. Seconds from now, we'll be in battle with actual vampires. I have no inkling how the power of the mind can subdue a strong, fast, thirsty creature like that, but I'm about to find out.

"See that?" Viesel Egos points at a bright spot

on the verge of tilting westward. He's reminding us that the sun is still shining. "Fawn, move the fog."

For the first time, I see the full strength of her power. Her force is robust, yet she has complete control of it, moving the vapors one molecule at a time. When she's done, there's not a stitch of fog in sight. About a hundred yards away, I see the three figures are on fire, quivering as their skin burns until they're ash heaps on the ground.

"Did you see how you did that?" he asks both of us, actually being helpful.

Sometimes, I swear Viesel can read my mind.

"Yes," we say at the same time.

"But did we have to kill them?" Fawn asks.

"Yes," Viesel Egos answers.

Without another word, he moves on, and so do we. After watching three vampires disintegrate into ashes, my alarm is up. Before, I was moving along as a spectator. Now, I am not. Fawn also appears to be on alert. She's pushed all the fog away. If more vampires were taking cover from the sun, then they too are now a pile of ashes. My mind hooks into Baron. He's still on the airplane, on the verge of bursting from being unable to be with us. The good thing is, he's not parched.

On the threshold of sundown, my energy

reaches the border of Ethiopia, far ahead of us. "Fawn, pull in."

She withdraws the force that she's been pushing out. I had questioned why Felix put instructions in me to fly into Cairo until we reached this point. *The evil* is whipping through the sky of Ethiopia, pulling supernatural border patrol.

"It's *the evil*," I say to Viesel Egos.

By the look on his face, he already knew they were there. "We go this way."

We follow him to the surface. I've been so tuned in to what's been happening in the air that I've hardly paid attention to the change in landscape on the ground. We stand at the edge of a purple mountain range with a late-day mist spread across the top of it. The valley is comprised of rich grasslands. A wall of trees border the jungle to the right of us. I feel life watching us, from the smallest insects to the largest four-footed animals.

Do you feel that? I ask Fawn.

I do, she answers, studying the thick tree line.

"It's your Life Blood," Viesel Egos says to both of our surprise.

I forgot he could hear us.

"Humans, they fear. You"—he looks at Fawn and me—"they do not."

The trees are rattling, and the birds are hawking, cooing, or singing from deep in the brush. The insects are buzzing too. It's strange, but their nearness is comforting. It's like being back in that place called Hope, which clearly we are not.

"Let's go," Viesel Egos says.

We start across the green valley, and I gaze at the sky. The sun has gone down. Minutes later, Baron is right beside me, holding my hand.

"That was fast," I say.

"Are you hurt?" He runs his other hand down my cheek and pulls back to inspect my body.

"No." I hug him.

Viesel Egos stops. "Keep up!"

Something about the way he looks at Baron tells me he does not disapprove of Baron being here. That's really odd, since Baron's a vampire, and Viesel Egos clearly hates them. I keep this thought in my head as we move along. There's a small farm at the base of the hill. We move up a dirt road toward the flat, dark shack, and I feel the protection over this place.

"Are we staying here tonight?" I ask Viesel Egos.

"No. Wait here." He takes off to the back of the shack.

"He's fine," Baron says to Fawn, who's been quiet for the majority of the journey.

"Thank you," she mouths.

"There was fog," I say to him.

"I know." He puts his arm around me, and I take Fawn's hand.

"Is she near?" I ask him.

He doesn't even hesitate. "Zina's here, but I'll deal with her."

"So she didn't burn in the sun?"

"Almost. She sent Magnus, Lucien, and Cyrus out before her."

"The three we saw burn into ashes?"

"Is that what happened to them?"

"I'm sorry," I say. "Did you know them?"

"Don't apologize. They were coming after you and Fawn."

"Are there more of them here?" I ask.

"The sun destroyed twelve of them. There are five left. Zina's making a big play, but you'll be safe once they're all dead."

"She didn't tell anyone else?"

"Telling too many vampires about the Life Blood is too dangerous. Remember what you saw in the tunnels?"

"I do." Although I try not to.

"They were toying with her. Those guys planned to kill me and her and come after you and Fawn."

"You chopped their heads off," I whisper.

He draws me closer. "My love, you are the preserver of life, not me."

I look at him with wide eyes. That's not exactly true at the moment. I've never wanted anything to die—not an ant, not even a vampire who wants to drain me dry—but Zina…I want her dead.

Headlights come our way. Viesel's behind the wheel of another Humvee, this one tan. The vehicle stops in front of us, the headlights power off, and the doors open. Fawn scoots into the front seat, and Baron and I take the backseats.

It's dark in the cab, and the road ahead of us is even darker. When Viesel turned off the headlights, he didn't turn them back on. Baron and I hold hands, but we're all silent, keeping our eyes open. At the border, we run right through a makeshift patrol station manned by men with Uzis. As I look out the back window, what I believe is confirmed. They can't see us because of the special brand of protection over the vehicle.

The road is bumpy, and we're deep in the jungle. Viesel Egos is going the right way; I see the path in my head as we bolt ahead. I want to feel what's out there, but I know I can't. But just because I can't feel what's out there doesn't mean I can't see it. Every now and then, a tree bends. I see flashes of a deeper black cut through the moon rays. Baron lets go of my hand and turns his entire body toward the window. I feel as if he's positioning himself to jump out. Though I want to stop him, I know if he chooses to go, there will be nothing I can do.

"What's going on?" I ask him.

"They're following us."

Viesel Egos's blue eyes are the only light in the cab, and he's staring at Baron. They're speaking to each other again, and I want to know what they're saying. The last time Viesel Egos talked in Baron's head, Baron left me. But no matter how hard I try, I cannot penetrate the shield that keeps me from getting inside Baron.

"What did he just say to you?" I finally ask Baron out of frustration.

Viesel Egos puts his eyes on me.

"Why don't you *talk* to me too, Viesel Egos? We're in this together." I'm on the edge of my seat.

Baron takes my hand again. "Hey, calm down."

"What's going on between you two?"

Before he can say anything, something slams hard into the vehicle. The Humvee just ran over a white figure that's now behind us, back on his feet, and charging after us. Fawn is already up with an arm stretched out over the back of her seat, and the figure is pinned to a tree. Before I can object, Baron jumps out the door. Moments later, he's back beside me. I focus on a dark speck on his chin. I touch it, and the tips of my fingers become wet with a dark substance. I'm sure it's blood.

"Four left?" I ask.

"Five." He's counting Zina.

We've been driving for about an hour. Every now and then, *the evil* hits us and we go zooming off the road, but Viesel Egos guides us back on. Pretty soon, we'll be near the burial site. All I can do is wonder how to get the job done. Since communicating isn't Viesel Egos's strong point, I'm pretty sure we'll have to think on our feet.

Somehow, we're going to have to dig up the grave while holding off *the evil*. We'll be sitting ducks for thirsty vampires. Basically, in a matter of minutes, it's all going to happen; I just hope we all come out alive.

CHAPTER

THIRTY

We zoom into the national park way after closing hours. It's pitch black, but I can smell the Blue Nile nearby. Zillael is buried three thousand, seven hundred fifty-five feet east, perpendicular to what is now called the Tis Issat Falls. The Humvee slows to a stop, and we all sit in silence. The gravity of what's about to happen even weighs on Viesel Egos.

"Is Fawn strong enough to push back *the evil?*" I ask him.

He sets his eyes on me. "Yes."

I touch Fawn's left shoulder and she cups her hand over mine.

"I'll start as soon as we're out," she says.

"Can you push in all four directions?"

"I think so."

"All right." I think some more before we head out. "Viesel?"

He looks at me.

"I haven't tried to influence *the evil* as of yet. Is there anything I can do to overwhelm it, or is this the Fawn show?"

"The Fawn show?" he asks, apparently confused by my wording.

I sigh and remember who I'm talking to. "I mean, is she the only one with the ability to battle back against *the evil*?"

"No. You can too."

"Okay...how?" *This conversation is ridiculous.* He should be the one briefing us.

"You have to get inside of it and fill it with the light."

"What light?"

"You have light," he says.

"I do?"

"Yes."

I take a deep breath, already weary. "Okay, I guess I'll find it within me then. And what about the grave?"

"That's me."

"Meaning, you're digging the grave?"

"Yes."

Baron is already keyed in to what's going on outside the vehicle. "Four more."

"Another vampire dead?" I ask.

"Pilot attacked Zina, and she was able to kill him before he killed her."

I don't know if they all feel as relieved as I do, but that's one more down.

"Let's go," Viesel Egos says.

Without another word, he's out of the driver's seat and on his way. Fawn exits, already pushing out her energy. Baron and I hop out next. All of my instincts are on high alert. There's no being overly cautious now. It's time to make sure we remain on the offense, never the defense. That's how battles are fought and won.

Black shadows dart over us a lot slower than before. Viesel Egos's sword of fire is engaged. The first black shadow dives at us, and with a clean swipe, he slices it in half. It lets out a high-pitched shriek, and he slices again and again. The cries are deafening. Baron has his silver blades engaged and is slicing too.

"Light!" Viesel Egos shouts.

Since I already know the way, I push the light out of me as I head east toward the gravesite. The light is remarkable. I wonder if those living nearby can see the light forcing its way up into the night. Just in case, I push out a shield of indifference as well.

Because of the light, we can see all around us as if it were early evening. I see a female in black running toward us at super speed. I know it's Zina, and I can feel her ice-cold, lifeless energy trained on me. When she tries to get close to me, she's sent flying into the trees by Fawn. Baron branches off to pursue her.

I want to follow him, but I know I can't stop moving forward. My sister has two years to live, and I have a book to find. That's all I can think about. I charge ahead, daring *the evil* to hit me with its best shot.

Viesel Egos's blade is working overtime. The cries of the wounded evil are unceasing. I feel the blackness hit me. It's trying to penetrate my shield of light, but the impact is like a cotton ball falling upon my face. My eyes are wide, and I see crystal clear. My steps are deliberate, and there's power in my legs. Up until now, the pushback has been weak. When we're only steps away from the gravesite, Fawn is knocked off her feet, and I struggle against a force five times stronger than the one I faced a few moments ago.

"Fawn, are you okay?" I shout, straining against *the evil*.

"I'm okay," she shouts.

A second later, she's standing right back beside me. We take each other's hand and squeeze. I see the dark trying to overwhelm me, but I'm feeding off of Fawn's energy. I feel the wind that's strong enough to bend trees pushing against me. My hair has blown out of the bun I keep it in. At first, the strands blow away from my face, but the more I focus on fighting this force, *the evil*, the more I feel my hair doing the impossible. Each strand is moving against the strong winds and shooting toward my face. I turn to Fawn, and her hair is doing the same thing. We're winning.

"Viesel, are you almost done?" I yell through the whooshing wind, flapping leaves, and bending branches.

I see him standing over the gravesite with those electric eyes bearing down over it. Millions of tiny particles of soil blast up from the ground and form a clean pile near the edge of a deep hole. He's actually using his eyes to shovel the dirt.

I know what we're searching for is near. I can

feel it. *The evil* is unrelenting. The deeper I go into it, the more visible it is to me. I see the corrosion of death itself in the form of millions of white skeletal faces with hollow black eyes and mouths that are blowing the wind we're battling.

"It's done," Viesel shouts.

It's time to walk and chew gum. The light is shooting out of my palms, but it's time to retrieve the book. I know its general location in the underground tomb.

I'm just about to make my move when I see two females charging at me from the left, and to the right, one male is charging toward Fawn. The ravenous looks on their faces tell me they're thirsty, and the first vampire to the Life Blood will drink us dry.

Fawn sees them too. She keeps one arm strong, palm aimed upward to battle *the evil*, and she shoots the other toward the two vampires flanking me. They're pinned to a tree long enough for Baron, who's moving with ease, to take his blade to them. They meet the same fate as the six vampires in the tunnel. I notice that Baron's glowing; light is pushing out of his pores. He jumps, flips over us, and takes his blade to the vampire to the right.

That's three, and not one of them is Zina. I'm

wondering where she is when an intense pain shoots through the lower right side of my back. I look down at my stomach and see the tip of a blade sticking out of me. My eyes expand. I'm bewildered by what's just happened to me.

I'm so hot.

I'm sweating.

I'm so dizzy.

I want to faint.

The pain brings me to my knees, but I'm determined to keep fighting. I push harder against *the evil*. I feel a struggle going on behind me. Baron is near, and he lets out a deafening, angry roar. It's not until I see Zina's head fly past me that I know who won.

I can't fight any longer. Both of my hands drop to the soil to hold me up. Baron kneels beside me.

"Clarity!" He sees the knife and sweeps me up.

He's running away with me. I know he's thinking that he has to save me somehow, but I have to make him take me back.

"Baron, no, stop!" I can't stop grimacing because the pain is so piercing. Even adrenaline can't stop the throbbing.

The light flashes inside him, aching to get out. I know he has to do what I can no longer do.

"You have to hold it off while I get the book," I shout, pulling on his shoulders.

He's still moving at record speed. "What the hell are you talking about? You've been injured, Clarity! I have to get you out of here!"

"Stop, Baron! Fawn can die! And that will kill me."

He stops dead in his tracks. "You can die too!"

"Just please take me back. I have to do this."

He's torn; I can read it all over his face. After a moment of deliberation, he darts back to the gravesite and puts me down next to Fawn. She's sweating profusely, but she's been successful at holding off *the evil* all by herself.

"Clarity, are you okay?" she shouts. I can tell by her expression that she's tortured.

"I'm fine!" I gasp. "I'm going in!"

Near the opening in the ground, Viesel Egos is working his blade like a madman. I wondered why he hadn't chased down Baron for carrying me off. It's because all hell is breaking loose around us. The light and dark are clashing above us.

"Shoot your palms up," I tell Baron.

He hesitates, but I can't wait around to see if he does what I ask. I crawl toward the grave. My breathing is labored, and the pain is piercing. The knife is still in me, but I cannot stop until I'm looking over an opened chamber about twenty feet deep into the earth. It looks like a deep drop, but then I remember I can walk on air.

I take a few deep breaths, put the pain in the back of my mind, and scoot off the edge of the grave. I drop down and concentrate on landing lightly on my feet. I feel blood draining from the open gash in my stomach and back. My head spins. My vision is blurry.

I turn in circles, mustering up enough strength to recall the exact location of the book. The scent of wet soil and death is all around me. Even in my current state, I'm amazed by this resting place that was built to house my grandmother's remains. It's the ultimate act of reverence by a son to his mother. I'm wondering what sort of grave Felix will build for me as I stumble to the table with what's left of Zillael's ancient bones. I drop to my knees and struggle to crawl under the dusty red silk cloth that covers the table. I know the book is under here somewhere.

After waddling around in a shallow pool of my own blood, I start to panic while losing faith. It's time to calm down and think. Then it hits me. I push light out of me and twist to see the bottom of the table. There it is, a script with thousands of lines of unique symbols. I drag myself to the edge of the table and scratch at the crevice to peel off the script. I'm left clutching one long sheet of something that feels more like cloth than paper.

The victory is in knowing that I have it. The despair is in knowing that I'm falling into unconsciousness.

CHAPTER

THIRTY-ONE

H ere's what I remember.

I heard Fawn screaming my name, urging me to stay with her. I heard Viesel Egos warn Baron to stay away from my blood, and Baron shouted that he didn't want my blood. Then I was swooped up and riding the wind. The dagger was still inside me until I reached a certain point, and then there was a sharp pain at my wound.

I see a blast of light as I slowly blink to consciousness. I'm lying in a bed, and a face I haven't seen in what feels like a few lifetimes is standing over me.

"Cl'auta, you are awake!" her sweet voice sings. She takes my hand and kisses my knuckles.

"Adore, I'm so happy to see you." My enthusiasm is in my smile, not my voice. I sound as though I'm just waking up.

"You were not vital when you arrived," she says.

"What happened?"

Then it all comes rushing back. I remember being stabbed in the back by a love-scorned vampire. I touch the spot where I was wounded, and it feels healed. I pull up the hem of my lightweight cotton dress, and there's not even a hint of a scar. Not that I'm surprised; strangely enough, I've never had a scar. That's just another weird thing I've ignored over the years.

"I'm back in Enu?" I already know the answer to that question.

"Yes, you are," Adore answers with a smile.

I look around the room. It's different than the one I was in last time. The walls are pure crystal, and other than the bed, there's no furniture. Beyond the walls, the sky is a pinkish blue with sprinkles of white. The sight is so intriguing that I hop out of bed to get a better view.

"And you are now fully recovered," Adore says with a giggle.

"It's so beautiful," I whisper with wonder. The flickering lights must be stars or planets. Then I remember that the last beautiful thing I saw was Baron Ze Feldis's face. He was begging me to wake up. *Don't die.* I whip around to ask, "Where's Baron?"

Adore's entire expression falls. "Do you mean the vampire?"

"Does he know I'm okay? Did someone tell him I'm alive?"

Still her face is blank.

"Where's Felix?" I ask. It's time to get on with the reason why I ended up here in the first place. More importantly, it's time I get back to Baron Ze Feldis.

"He is in the second sphere."

"Could you take me to him?"

"Now?" she asks.

"Please?"

"You are leaving so soon?" She looks so sad.

I grimace, hating the fact that my decision causes her such unhappiness. "I must."

Adore puts on a lovely smile and steps up to me with an outstretched hand. I take her hand, and as quick as a blink, we're off.

Like Adore, I can go right through the walls. As we soar in the cotton candy-colored sky, I gaze at the land below. The silver, pink, and crystal trees are part of the real Enu, but I also see crystal roads running along the streams and rainbows hovering over roaring waterfalls.

There's a valley of purple rocks surrounded by an emerald-green mountain range. We race over a city that looks a lot like the one I saw before. The only difference is this one has actual beings in it. I see fruit stands in what looks to be a bustling outdoor marketplace. Shockingly, real Enuians don't wear clothes; they are totally naked. The funny thing is that I don't react to their exposed state. It seems as natural as breathing and as freeing as the wind. Their bodies are slightly different than human bodies, but we're moving so fast, I have no time to figure out what that difference is.

I follow Adore through a partition of water and into a cave where the walls, the ceiling, and the floor are made of a substance that looks like gold. Even more remarkable is that it's daylight in here, but there's no sun in sight. It appears the rays of the Enu sun can flow through inanimate objects. There are Enuians down here too, nude and carrying buckets of water on their shoulders. I notice the difference between them and me; the women do not have breasts.

"I will show you something," Adore says. She

skips off to the pool of water where there's a golden shelf holding a line of golden cups. She takes one and dips it into the pool. She hands me the cup of water. "Drink it."

I hesitate but drink all of it. I feel the coolness flow down my throat, and the flavor is like nothing I've ever tasted. I can't even explain its pure deliciousness. "Wow!"

"Give it some time to work."

"What's going to happen?"

She giggles. "We will have to see, Cl'auta. It all depends on you."

I smile at her. It's nice to see her this way. Then the effect hits me. My whole body feels refreshed, as though every nerve is sucking on a mint. Any thirst I may have had is quenched, and I feel as though I'll never need to drink another glass of water.

"I think it worked," she says in awe.

"Well, I surely felt something."

"This is really good, Cl'auta. Do you know what this means?" Her entire face lights up. "You're already part of this universe. You're truly more Enuian than human."

"Like you?"

She gives me her tight-lipped smile, and I know what that means. Adore is withholding information and has decided not to say anything more on the subject. Because I respect her reasons for doing so, I don't pressure her.

"There is the entrance," she says, pointing behind me.

I look over my shoulder toward the entryway. "You're not coming?"

"These things are not for me to know at this time."

I recall the journey, the battle with evil, and seeing vampires, creatures that were once human, getting killed. The blood, the death, the dark—these are not things that are part of Adore's life.

"Will you ever visit the earth?" I ask her. If she and I are sisters, then she has to be a quarter human too.

"Never."

"Can you tell me why?"

She grins broadly as she points toward the portal again. "Father is calling you. You must leave."

I turn to the narrow fissure. We hug good-bye until next time, and I walk through the tight gap. A flash of light engulfs me, and I'm standing on a wooden deck overlooking the crystal sea. Felix is sitting on a wiry bench with no legs. I can reasonably conclude that it's literally suspended in midair. I also conclude that this is not the same deck we visited the last time we met in Enu.

When he sees me, he stands. "I see you're up."

"Yes, miraculously, I'm all healed. It must be Enu."

That was a leading statement. I'm hoping Felix will elaborate more on why I feel brand new after losing all of that blood, not to mention the internal injuries. He just stands there looking at me. It's strange, but from the twinkle in his eyes, I think my father is overjoyed to see me up and walking.

"You succeeded in securing the writings and getting them to me," he finally says.

"Yes." I walk over to the bench. "Can you tell me exactly what happened afterward?"

"Egos brought you to the gateway, and I brought you in." He glares out over the crystal sea. "Thank your vampire the next time you see him."

"Is Baron okay?

"Yes, he is."

"And Fawn?"

"She survived."

I nod, picturing the last time I saw her. She had expended every ounce of energy to battle *the evil*, and when I fell, the pain of the blade shooting through me, she battled it alone until Baron took my place. It all seems so long ago. Then I remember…

"How long have I been here in Earth days?"

Felix frowns. "Come with me."

There really isn't any place to go but into the water. As Felix gets to the edge of the platform, the wood builds out as we go, extending for him into the crystal-clear sea. At first the depth of the water is ankle-high. It's the perfect temperature—cool but not cold. As we move forward, the water reaches knee-high, then waist-high. After a few more steps, I hold my breath because we're about to be completely submerged.

When I'm under the water, I let out my breath. There's no need to hold it; I can actually breathe underwater. It feels strange, as if this is impossible and can't be really happening. There's a whole other world underwater. On one side, I see schools of black and white fish, some type of green fish with grassy skin, and gold fish that are actually gold, not orange. I turn to see what's on the other side of me and find dunes made of pearl. I'm so enthralled that I almost miss seeing Felix take a sharp left turn.

We enter a cozy room, of course designed in my father's tastes of hard white leather, straight angles, and glass. There's a smaller chamber attached, and we head back there. In the middle of the room is a massive block that looks like a table. In a flash, I see myself peeling the sheet from the bottom of the platform where Zillael's bones rest.

"It wasn't a book," I say, finally remembering.

"No, it's a scroll made of papyrus," Felix says.

I walk over to study the sheet with Felix. There are rows of symbols and tiny drawings written in a peculiar script.

"Did you write this?" I ask.

"No. When Zillael was alive, she was shown the future and given the words to write."

"Who showed her the future?"

"They're called angels on Earth."

I take a closer look at the scroll. "What language is this?" Interpreting this writing is proving difficult.

"It's the first language ever spoken by humankind."

"That's amazing." I'm still attempting to figure out the first few words. "Seven seeds."

"That's good, Cl'auta." Felix squeezes my shoulder, his way of showing he's proud of me. When I graduated from Harvard both times, he squeezed my shoulder. "This script contains the prophecy of the seven seeds."

"Are you able to translate the writings?" I ask.

"I am, but the one of the seven who has the power of the mind can, and that's you."

"Why me?"

Felix runs his hand across the first line and stops on a tiny drawing of a female with tons of hair and tiny etchings circling her head, representing the sun. "This is you, Cl'auta."

"Ultimate wisdom," I whisper, surprised I figured that out. "At this point, I'm supposed to have ultimate wisdom."

"That was also my conclusion."

Then I remember something Adore told me. "You're able to encase too. Does this mean you have the power of the mind?"

"I have all seven powers," he says. "Each of you inherits your power from me. The power of the mind is the most dominant."

I think about that while studying the bottom half of the sheet. None of it makes sense yet. Then I move back up to the first line. Slowly, I establish that a boy will grow up with the powers of mind, force, fire, light, strength, speed, and matter.

"Light...that's Adore?"

"She is the light."

"That's why she refuses to go to Earth," I guess.

"She will one day. She has to."

I frown at him, perplexed.

"Keep going," he says.

I slide a finger across the scroll. "You're obviously the boy." I glance at him. "You became a man and fell in love with one from that place called Hope." When I glance at him again, he keeps his eyes down. Something is going on inside him, but I'm sure I'll never be able to encase or sense him, so I don't even try. I continue deciphering. "She'll be impregnated by his human seed and have seven daughters. And there I am." I move down farther. "There's the leaf. There's Fawn." My heart jumps out of my chest.

Felix stares at me. His eyes are speaking to me, and I get the message.

"How long have I been in here in Earth time?" I ask again.

"She has three days left."

"And you didn't take the leaf out of Lario?"

Felix fixes his eyes on me. His teeth are clenched. "I tried."

"Did something happen?"

"I almost killed him—and Falu."

"I don't understand."

"I'm more human than you. I almost ripped out Falu's heart along with his."

"I have to do it?"

"Yes. And bring me the leaf." He points at a symbol on the scroll. "See?"

I do see.

Felix touches my temples. "Here's the eye, Cl'auta. You'll be able to see the portals and the protection from this moment on. No one needs to bring you to them. You'll find the entries on your own."

Across the room, on the wall near the entrance to this chamber, I see where to make my exit.

THIRTY-TWO

I end up in the forest surrounding Fawn and Lario's house. It's nighttime, but I can see so much more with these new eyes of mine. The protection still sprayed against the sky looks like a net of fire, but there are huge gaps in it. The largest breach leaves the entire house exposed.

The sun has just dropped to the west, and it's getting dusky in the woods. There's enough protection over the yard to keep the vampires from lingering, but I sense strong thirst on the outskirts of the mangled protection. Hundreds of them are out there, waiting to seize the Life Blood. The field is being watched as well. So I think *blind* and push that energy out over the entire diameter of the protection—except the gap over the house.

My senses picked up something else. Fawn's life force isn't strong, but Lario's is coming in loud and clear. Since they're linked, that seems odd. My intuition is screaming *beware* and makes me shudder more than all of the other chilling conditions combined.

I move quickly across the field and walk through the unlocked front door. The silence and stillness is eerie. Blocking out Lario, I call for Fawn while moving through the reading room and then the kitchen, which is also abandoned. She doesn't answer, but a muddled sign of her comes through.

The old me would've run around the entire house, searching every room for her. Instead, I zero in on Lario's energy. He's not upstairs or on the primary level. He actually comes in stronger beneath the foundation of the house. Of course there's an underground level. How else could Baron escape during the daylight?

Keep watch are the instructions I leave myself as I send my life force out to search for Lario, hoping he'll lead me to Fawn.

I cut through the soil, marking the scent of damp earth. Lario's energy rings loud and clear. I wind up in a dim room where Fawn is curled up against the wall, lying on the cold cement floor. Her skin is pale, actually winter-white. My heart explodes. This is what pure rage must feel like. I want to think *death* to see if that kills him on the spot. But deep within me lives the desire to preserve life, and that makes Lario a lucky man.

Fawn senses me and lifts her head about an inch off the ground. That one action appears to be a chore. *She's so weak.* I wrap her in my energy, giving her as much of my vitality as she can take in these brief seconds. I see the two small holes on her neck. The wounds are scabbing, but I'm quite sure a vampire has been drinking her.

I study the walls of the room. They're made of silver, and silver chains hang in the entryway. This is clearly a prison, designed to contain her and keep out vampires. Her captor is right beyond the chain link door.

I'll be back, I whisper to her and her only.

She whimpers, which is good. She's making a sound; that lets me know she's recovering.

The area outside of Fawn's prison looks like a regular white chamber lit by dim blue lighting. Lario is on a cot, and another male—I can only see his back—stands over him.

The other guy has short-cropped, messy brown hair, and he keeps glancing over his shoulder at the silver chains in the doorway. "You said you were going to take those down before I change you back."

"I'll take it down after you change me."

As I figured, the guy's a vampire.

"You can't touch silver when you're a vampire. You know that, Exgesis."

Lario sits up. "I have it covered. Just do it, and you get the Life Blood and I get to be a vampire again."

The vampire rubs his hands together, deliberating. Then he's right in Lario's face. "I should kill you right now!"

Lario is as cavalier as ever. He jumps to his feet. "Kill me. Then you'll be stupid enough to make sure you *don't* taste one ounce of the Life Blood."

Again, the vampire checks over his shoulder. He's so greedy for Fawn, and it sickens me.

"Don't you remember how that taste of her made you feel? No thirst. You could kill a whole host of your enemies with one swipe. You want to throw that away because you can't trust a squirt like me?"

The vampire sinks his teeth into Lario's jugular. After a moment, with a loud howl, he pulls his mouth from Lario's neck. He scratches down on his own neck until he's bleeding. It's time for Lario to drink.

Now it's I who's snarling. I've had enough, so without delay, I shoot into Lario's heart. Lario hits the floor, clutching the left side of his chest. It's dark in here, which makes it easier to see the green leaf. It glows bright, lodged in a withered, sooty heart that hasn't beaten in hundreds of years. Without further ado, I snatch it out of him.

The leaf falls on the floor because without my physical body, I can't carry it. Lario knows just what happened. Even while convulsing, he reaches for the leaf, but the leaf forces his hand away. When the other vampire looks at it, he's blinded by it.

I sense Fawn behind me. She's stepped out from behind the silver chains, exposing herself to this thirsty vampire who thinks he just hit the lottery. He thinks he's about to kill two trapped weasels at one time because Lario's down and the Life Blood just walked out of the silver-plated prison.

Before he can reach Fawn, she raises a palm, and the force of her untamed power takes his head right off. Then she aims her palm at Lario, who's doubled over and wailing.

He finds enough strength to look at Fawn and

reach toward her. "Don't! I was doing this for the both of us!"

Fawn looks conflicted, and a flood of tears gush down her cheeks. Regardless of all he's done to her, she doesn't want to harm him.

Put him in the room. We'll deal with him later, I tell her.

Like a rag doll in the wind, he flies into the room and slams against the wall.

Can you get out of here, or do I have to come get you? I ask her.

She lifts a weak arm toward a steel door. *Elevator.*

I see the leaf still on the ground. *Can you get the leaf?*

It's a struggle, but she nods.

All of me is back in the kitchen. I rush into the reading room just in time to see one of the bookcases pull apart. Two shiny steel doors pull open.

"Cl'auta," Fawn mutters as she stumbles out of the elevator and collapses into my arms.

The leaf falls out of her hand and glides onto the wooden floor. I have to get her to Enu, but first, I secure the leaf. Since there are no pockets on the white cotton dress I'm wearing, I have to shove it into my bra. We drag across the yard. Strangely, she's quite heavy, like dead weight. I'm huffing and puffing and fearing our progress is too slow.

"Fawn," I call over and over.

She's woozy and unable to respond beyond a weak moan. Then Baron Ze Feldis appears out of nowhere and swipes Fawn out of my arms. We stand face to face, and I'm lost for words. Two years have passed. He's as pale as chalk, and the deep purple indentures under his eyes tell me he's parched.

"You're better," he mutters.

"I am." Part of me wants to cling to him and tell him how much I love him and how good it is to see him alive. But Fawn needs my help.

"I'll help you," he says.

We're able to move faster across the field and into the woods. We come to a grinding halt near the portal.

"I'll take it from here." As I take Fawn, who's completely unconscious, my arm rubs Baron's; he's arctic cold.

The leaves crackle under his feet as he steps back.

"Meet me in Manhattan?" I ask him. I'm a little skittish about where we stand because he's keeping his distance.

He doesn't say a word. Instead, he turns and takes off, leaving me staring at the empty space he left behind. Part of me wants to chase him. But after gazing down at Fawn's pale, lifeless face, I rush into the portal.

In Enu, Fawn is feather-light. In my head, I call for Adore. When we reach Felix's flat where the book is kept, she's at the entrance ready to receive Fawn. But to my surprise, Felix steps up in front of Adore to take her instead. He shoots off so fast that it almost looks as if he's disappeared into thin air.

"This way," Adore says, already moving.

I follow her through a series of different portals until we're back in the chamber with the crystal glass walls and bed. Fawn is already lying on top of the bed, and Felix is standing over her. His mouth is open, and he's blowing light into Fawn's mouth and nostrils. She's glowing like a night-light.

Adore moves over to me. "The vampire who did this to her, is he still alive?"

"For now."

My intention for Lario is indicated in my tone, but when Adore takes my hand, I'm filled by her influence until I want to take those feelings back.

"What is Felix doing?" I ask.

"She has lost a lot of her light over the years,

and when the vampire drank her, he almost sent her to the dark world."

"Where's that?"

"I do not know exactly."

When Felix is done, he kisses Fawn's forehead, which is a demonstration of affection I didn't think he was capable of performing.

"She'll be good as new," he says to me. "Do you have the leaf?"

I turn to fish it out of its hiding place, and I hand it to him.

"You said Lario isn't dead. Is he contained?" he asks.

"Fawn put him in the same prison he kept her in. Apparently it keeps vampires out, so I imagine it'll keep one in too."

"Is he now a Selell?"

I take a moment to ponder that. "I think so."

Felix flexes his jawbone. "I'll be back." He moves out quickly through the portal.

CHAPTER

THIRTY-THREE

T
ime ticks by on Enu, and on Earth, the days stack up. Baron Ze Feldis stays in the forefront of my mind, but I have to trust our love can survive this distance. I can't leave until Fawn is fully recovered. As we wait, Adore and I only leave her bedside to dine in the main room. More fruits are added to our feast, some I've never known existed. There's one called a *tep* that looks like a pomegranate, but the juice-filled seeds are blue and taste like baked apples. The tep is now my favorite food.

"Are you still in love with the vampire?" Adore asks out of nowhere as we sit at Fawn's bedside.

"I am," I admit. "But something's very different."

"In you or him?"

"In him. He helped me carry Fawn into the woods, but he was really distant. Something must've happened. I just don't know what."

"Cl'auta," Fawn whispers.

Adore and I leap out of our seats to stand over her.

"You're back!" I brush her forehead gently.

A healthy, rosy undertone is set in her skin; she's always been so pale. Fawn sits up and looks at me with the saddest eyes. "I'm so sorry, Cl'auta. I couldn't stop Lario."

"You don't have to apologize for not being able to fend off a monster."

"He's not a monster," she quickly but tenderly retorts.

I give her a tight-lipped smile. That's how she feels, but not me. He knew all along she would die, which means his plans were premeditated and self-serving. That makes him, if not a monster, a very bad individual.

"He told Ze Feldis that you fell in love with Viesel Egos and chose to stay here in Enu with him forever," Fawn says.

"Why would he say that?" I'm ready to race off and defend myself to Baron.

"You sound so sad, Cl'auta," Adore says.

"Well, I am."

"Ze Feldis showed up every day waiting for you to return," Fawn continues. "I think Lario wanted him gone so he could…" She stops short.

We fall silent. The moment is heavy, but the sky is pink and holds never-ceasing twinkling lights. The mountain range on the horizon is composed of diamond rock. There's nothing but beauty, peace, and deep love here. I don't want to disturb it.

"Fawn, what happened? How did you end up where I found you?" I ask.

She looks through the window, maybe drawing hope from the crystal-clear mountain range. "He started poisoning my food with *mirk*…"

Adore gasps, and my eyes dart over to her.

"What's mirk?"

"Human blood. We should never drink it *ever*," Adore warns.

"It took only one dose to incapacitate me. When I asked him why, he didn't say anything. There was nothing in his eyes. He was just blank."

"He's a sociopath," I blurt. My entire face is frowning.

"Don't say that," Fawn says, still defending him.

"Well, what else can you call it?"

"He's injured."

"Okay…" Cynicism colors my tone.

Fawn and Adore give each other a look.

"She has the power of the mind," Adore says to Fawn. Then she turns to me. "You know too much about the thoughts and hearts of creatures to believe there is hope for even the darkest soul. But Cl'auta, hurts can be healed, dark made light. Remember that."

Fawn smiles, and they take each other's hands. Deep down, I wish to connect with them on that level. It's not impossible, but right now, I'm not there.

"Fawn, Adore, I have to go." I'm lightheaded, but I find enough bearings to stand steadily.

"We know," Fawn says.

"Yes," Adore concurs.

Before leaving, I look over my shoulder at Adore. "And I'll remember."

THIRTY-FOUR

It's very late in the afternoon when I arrive in Manhattan. I choose to take off the light cotton dress of Enu and put on the clothes I was wearing the day we recovered the script. There's no fog, which means the vampires aren't lurking. Just in case, I spread a protective force of blindness over myself.

New York hasn't changed. Car horns honk, engines purr, and brakes screech. It's cold. Rain clouds congregate above. I used to love this time of year because it's dark enough to get a preview of what the night will look like. Right now, I'm betraying my old self.

The streets are too wide and congested with traffic and pedestrians. Too many people are pounding the pavement. I'm looking at them all differently because I know there are forces in this world that want to change their humanity. Most of them choose not to let those forces devour them, but what about the vulnerable ones? Deep down, I know I've been created for the vulnerable. Baron was just that when he walked into that tavern and gave up his humanity. *Injured*, Fawn called it. Now look at him. He used light to battle *the evil*.

I'm sure a lot more time has passed since Baron helped me carry Fawn into the woods. I stop at a newspaper stand and dig out the wallet I stuffed in my pocket years ago. I buy the day's issue of the *New York Times*. Another year has passed.

When I get to my old apartment, nothing has changed. It's just as I left it. One of the white clay mugs that I molded for myself still sits on top of the breakfast nook. I twist and turn it to study my handiwork, and then I take a sniff. It still smells like peppermint tea. It's been forever since I sculpted or molded anything. I don't even feel like an artist anymore. But this cup is simply gorgeous. I did good work.

I put the cup back down and move to the window. There are the buildings I've been in love with for five years: the glass-walled ones, salmon-brick ones, steel-plated cement ones, and so many more varieties. Nothing has changed for them, but everything has changed for me. I frown at my old friends, saying good-bye. They don't move me in the same way anymore, and there's something sad about that. What isn't sad is having Baron Ze Feldis in my life. I'm sure he senses that I'm back, and soon he'll be here.

Before sundown, I shower and wash my hair, which is a chore in itself. I haven't lost one strand in the last three years. The good thing is it doesn't take long to dry, which has always been sort of strange. I'm pretty sure there's an out-of-this-world explanation for it. I slip into my royal blue tank dress and— strangely enough—check myself in the mirror. I return to the window to gaze out over the city and to wait for him.

It's officially nighttime, but there's still no sign of Baron Ze Feldis. I look over my shoulder at the door. Where's his quiet knock? I open the door, hoping to be surprised by him standing there, but there's not a soul in the hallway. The lit skyscrapers beyond the windows are closing in on me. The only way to break out of this container is to find Baron.

When I find him, he's at the Metropolitan Museum of Art, shuffling up the stacked steps with a tall, beautiful woman on his arm. She doesn't look human. I don't sense that she has a soul, so I'm sure she isn't. He's wearing a black tuxedo, and she's in a strappy black dress that shows off her narrow curves. Other partygoers in their suits and cocktail dresses pass right through me. I stand at the bottom of the steps. My eyes are trained on the back of Baron's head.

Look, I think.

He stops in his tracks and whispers in his companion's ear. She searches over both shoulders but doesn't connect eyes with me. I'm not sure what he told her, but she walks on without him. Baron turns slowly to glare at me. I'm not sure what his expression means, but it's wide and sort of sad.

How's Fawn? he asks.

With that, I rush my bodiless self up the steps. We're standing face to face.

She's better than before, I say.

We just stare at each other. I have a million questions to ask him, but the most dominant takes precedence over the others.

What's going on between you and me? I ask.

He opens his mouth to speak, but then stops himself.

You know what Lario told you about Viesel Egos and me was just a bold-faced lie. Right?

Yes, he says in a strained voice.

So you're not hurt or mad at me because of that?

Of course not, Clarity. I know...knew— Again he stops short.

What's going on, Baron? Are you bonded with her? I glance up to signify the woman I saw him with.

After a moment, he says, *I am.*

But why? What about me? What about us? I sound too sad and sort of pathetic.

Clarity, I must go inside, but have a good, safe life.

I've been hit by a two-ton boulder. My heart aches so much that the pain leaves me struggling to breathe. I can't look at his face any longer, so I focus on the line of black limousines unloading their passengers. I won't plead for our love, but I do have one more question.

Did you know what Lario did to Fawn? My tone is much stiffer. I still refuse to look at him.

By the time I learned what he'd done to her, it was too late.

With that, I turn away and return to myself, dragging my heavy limbs into the bedroom. The first round of tears and sobbing hits me hard. My pillow becomes soaking wet.

Warmth surrounds me, and joy replaces the pain in my heart. There's a kiss on my forehead, cheek, and lips.

"Baron," I whisper, and my eyes open. I'd fallen asleep. That must've been a dream.

The clock on the nightstand says it's six thirty in the evening. I must've been asleep for a very long time. My pillow is bone-dry. Too bad my heartache couldn't dry up like that. I know one thing for sure —it's time to return to Enu.

I shuffle through my closet until I find a pair of black slacks that look comfortable enough. I pick through my shoes and find a pair of black Oxfords, purchased by Freda, of course. I find a black tank top and throw on a black pea coat. Black's the perfect color to wear while grieving.

I stop at the door to take in my apartment one last time. I can never return here nor to Cambridge. There are too many confusing memories in both places. From this point on, there's only one direction to look—ahead.

THE COMPLETE PARCHED SERIES

Book 1 - Parched
Book 2 - The Seventh Sister
Book 3 - Quenched
Book 4- The Fifth Sister
Book 5 - Ignite
Book 6 - Light Speed
Book 7 - Vanqush

PARCHED SERIES NOVELS

Steal With A Kiss
Forget Me Never

www.ingramcontent.com/pod-product-compliance
Lightning Source LLC
Chambersburg PA
CBHW050659290626
47170CB00016B/2476